PRAISE FOR

How Not to Read

"I wish this book had come out years ago, so that I could have avoided going to college and skipped straight to the bright and shiny life of a stand-up comedian. My eyes have been opened. My mind has been closed."

—Kumail Nanjiani, comedian, *Franklin and Bash*

"As an author as well as the daughter of a librarian, this book ought to enrage me. However, it actually gives me a throbbing ladyboner. This book has everything I want in my reading experience: hilarity, intelligence, swear words, Photoshop, and occasional doses of homoerotica. It made me feel better about pretending to be an avid reader, and it's helping me maintain my status as a faux-intellectual. Thanks, Dan!"

—Sara Benincasa, author of *Agorafabulous! Dispatches from My Bedroom*

"I used to lament never having gone to college, but no more! Thanks to Dan Wilbur's hilarious and handy guidebook, I can talk to artsy-fartsy educated types with confidence."

—Kambri Crews, author of *Burn Down the Ground: A Memoir*

"God bless Dan Wilbur and his noble crusade to free us from the tyranny of literacy. Finally, after all these years, we can say it: Suck it, Johannes Gutenberg!"

—Christian Finnegan, comedian

continued . . .

"Dan Wilbur is an amazingly educated human being, and funnier than his education should allow. It's nice to see him put those two things together into a book where the latter trumps the former. Bonus: I have responses other than 'I read that a long time ago so I don't remember specifics' when asked about the classics at parties."

—Emily Gordon, comedy producer and host, "The Indoor Kids"

"This is the smart, funny, charming book I have been desperate for since the day I first saw the Better Book Titles Tumblr and shouted at my coworkers 'Tumblr Book Deal! I'm so calling it! This guy is getting a Tumblr book deal!' I like being right, but I like Dan Wilbur's sense of humor even more."

—Rachel Fershleiser, editor of the *New York Times* bestselling
Six-Word Memoir series

"If you ever thought reading was a good idea, *How Not to Read* will show you how just very wrong you've been."

—Marie Cloutier, BostonBibliophile.com

BETTER BOOK TITLES PRESENTS

HOW NOT TO READ

Harnessing the Power of a Literature-Free Life

DAN WILBUR

A PERIGEE BOOK

A PERIGEE BOOK
Published by the Penguin Group
Penguin Group (USA) Inc.
375 Hudson Street, New York, New York 10014, USA

Penguin Group (Canada), 90 Eglinton Avenue East, Suite 700, Toronto, Ontario M4P 2Y3, Canada
(a division of Pearson Penguin Canada Inc.) • Penguin Books Ltd., 80 Strand, London WC2R 0RL,
England • Penguin Group Ireland, 25 St. Stephen's Green, Dublin 2, Ireland (a division of Penguin
Books Ltd.) • Penguin Group (Australia), 250 Camberwell Road, Camberwell, Victoria 3124, Australia
(a division of Pearson Australia Group Pty. Ltd.) • Penguin Books India Pvt. Ltd., 11 Community
Centre, Panchsheel Park, New Delhi—110 017, India • Penguin Group (NZ), 67 Apollo Drive,
Rosedale, Auckland 0632, New Zealand (a division of Pearson New Zealand Ltd.) • Penguin Books
(South Africa) (Pty.) Ltd., 24 Sturdee Avenue, Rosebank, Johannesburg 2196, South Africa
Penguin Books Ltd., Registered Offices: 80 Strand, London WC2R 0RL, England

While the author has made every effort to provide accurate telephone numbers, Internet addresses,
and other contact information at the time of publication, neither the publisher nor the author assumes any
responsibility for errors, or for changes that occur after publication. Further, the publisher does not have any
control over and does not assume any responsibility for author or third-party websites or their content.

First edition: September 2012

Library of Congress Cataloging-in-Publication Data

Wilbur, Dan.
How not to read : hamessing the power of a literature-free life / Dan Wilbur.
p.   cm.
ISBN 978-0-399-53761-5 (pbk.)
1. Books—Humor.   2. Books and reading—Humor.   I. Title.
PN6231.B62W55   2012
818'.5402—dc23   2012017470

PRINTED IN THE UNITED STATES OF AMERICA

10   9   8   7   6   5   4   3   2   1

Most Perigee books are available at special quantity discounts for bulk purchases for sales
promotions, premiums, fund-raising, or educational use. Special books, or book excerpts,
can also be created to fit specific needs. For details, write: Special Markets, Penguin Group
(USA) Inc., 375 Hudson Street, New York, New York 10014.

CONTENTS

Getting to the Point

No one has time to read anymore. I didn't even take the time to profred this bokk. But here's my promise to you: If you can get through even some of this book, you'll never have to read another book for the rest of your life! Instead of slogging through blurbs and back cover synopses, you can pretend to have read the greatest literary works of all time just by running your vacant eyes over a few of the next two hundred pages!

And this can benefit everyone . . . including:

1. People who never read
2. People who read sparingly
3. People who live to read, and vice versa

For people who have never read, this book is of the utmost importance. Everyone you know, even if you're sure they only crack open a book once a century, will judge your intellect based on how you discuss what you've read. Consider this a guide to finding and forgetting your first and last book. The best course of action is to read this book in its entirety, then act as if you've read everything ever put on paper, even though you spend all your free time correctly: doing anything except reading.[1]

For people who occasionally read, this book will stop you from constantly bringing up *New York Times* articles at dinner parties. Now you'll be able to discuss old novels instead of repeating vague, half-remembered facts about a moderately famous ballet dancer who just died.

For people who read all the time, this book may serve as a long, humbling list of those works you'll never finish. But, never fear. With enough rereads of this book you can continue to look down on every person you meet and take comfort in exclaiming "Really?! You've never even heard of [insert esoteric novel]?" because I will teach you how to talk down to other snobs without so much as a glance at the works those snobs recommend! Their taste will not hold a candle to yours, so never feel tempted to follow anyone else's reading advice but mine. You'll win every time, Smartypants. Now back to your friendless reading cave with you! *Ouch. |=⊂*

Betterbooktitles.com, a website I created, is devoted to summing up all of literature with fake, more accurate covers for each book, so you, dear person pretending to be a reader, do not have to read another stupid book again. This book takes that site one step further, providing you with even more techniques to fake your way through the classics and the not-so-classics. But just in case you're about to stop reading this book right now, here is what you'll also gain from its contents:

---

1. For a complete list of what to do besides reading, see pages 8–11.

- People are pompous dicks about reading.
- Books are not as fun as other media.
- I, Dan Wilbur, am an extremely lonely person with a lot of spare time.

It's time to stop fearing those people who keep bringing up Ayn Rand when you've never read a lick of her work. You no longer need to waste countless minutes on Wikipedia or SparkNotes catching up on your reading. It's okay if you don't want to give up one hundred–plus hours per week to peruse gargantuan nonfiction bestsellers, the Bible, and other books you've been claiming to have read since eighth grade.

In *How Not to Read*, you'll find tips for getting through anything you have to read by reading faster (just read every third word![2]), entire genres summed up in a single page (Historical Fiction: "Guess who else had sex: Hitler!"[3]), and how to spot a phony who claims to read incessantly when he has read exactly one book.[4] While this book is devoid of any "content" in the conventional sense, it will help you appear smarter and more appealing to people who are way out of your league.[5] And who better to give the gist of every canonical text than a comedian with

---

2. *One Hundred Years of Solitude* becomes: "Many as the Colonel was, that when him ice." Wow! It's like a Gertrude Stein poem only more comprehensible! *Moby-Dick* becomes: "Ishmael." You get the general idea!

3. Spoiler alert: He liked weird stuff.

4. Ten years ago. Usually *The Catcher in the Rye* or *To Kill a Mockingbird*.

5. Quick tip: Place a bookmark on page 165 so it always appears that you're just about done with the book. Carry it around in public! That's sure to start up a conversation. Unless you're reading this on a Kindle, in which case, you're free to attend a Kindle Meetup group, which I'm assuming is a lot like a key party, except you put your Kindle in the bowl instead of your keys.

a Classics degree who spent most of his time in college smoking pot and playing Super Mario Galaxy?

So, slackers of the world: unite! Long books will be vanquished! Bad books will be tarnished! And we will all breathe a sigh of relief as we make this retort to some snotty, overeducated dolt: "Yes, I have read *Ulysses*. It ends with an awesomely long sex scene."

UGHHH! Books Are the Worst!

Reading is hard but rewarding.

Oh, wait—I'm sorry! I thought I was talking to five-year-olds who have never seen TV or the outside of their secret-backyard-kidnap-sheds. Reading is actually worthless and inane.[1] The last book that mattered was *The Odyssey*, and at the height of Homer's popularity people hired blind guys to sing the words to them. That's how boring reading is! The Greeks didn't even like it, and they were into

---

1. Other things that are more entertaining than reading include: staring at a candle, staring at a wall, and staring off into the distance at nothing in particular. By the way, this is a footnote. Everything funny in this book will appear down here because it's impossible for me to be funny about one subject for more than a page without putting a non sequitur about poop down here. Ha! Poop is funny. It's funny that people poop.

everything boring.[2] I can't think of anything as boring as reading, and I've seen Noam Chomsky speak in person.[3]

Books are lengthy one-way conversations. Think about it: If you met your favorite book in a bar, he'd be the most annoying, long-winded jerk there. Even if your favorite book is a Bukowski novel, you'd just sit there with him, listening to hour after hour of stories about other times he drank and felt sad, until you both wanted to kill yourselves.[4]

Some smart dude once said books are "mirrors walking down the road," but I would add that books are more like mirrors walking down the road telling you you're dumb if you're not interested in what the mirror is saying. Books are judgmental of everything you do, and instead of simply telling you you're fat the way regular mirrors do, books tell you why your soul is weak and empty.

Another smart guy once said that art holds up a mirror to nature. That's why art will always be better than books: Art serves a practical purpose. Certain sculptures and frames can hold up mirrors. But books keep walking around with their weird mirror-faces like the death figure in a Maya Deren film,[5] taunting you into reading what's inside them. With their blurbs and their colorful jackets, books will be the first to tell you how interesting they think they are. Well, fuck you, books! I'm not interested in you at all! You think you're so special with your ideas and

---

2. Stargazing, politics, bathing.

3. I said it!

4. He's also the only book that would try to borrow money from you to bet on a horse race.

5. If you're really trying to look smart without reading, tell everyone you love the "etherealness" of Maya Deren's short films. They'll have no idea what you're referencing, much the same way as you have no idea what I'm referencing here. Who is smarter now? Answer: none of us.

relatable stories concerning the human condition! What can I learn from you that I couldn't learn from conspiracy theory videos on the Internet? Probably nothing. Books have information but aren't entertaining at all. If they were really trying to get people's attention, they would all have naked pictures on their covers and be made from smokable hemp.[6] Books are boring. QED.

You may be wondering, *If books are so boring and terrible, why do people keep saying I should read more books?* Simple: The elite who control the world want you to read more so you become stupid but think you're smart. Forcing people to like books is a conspiracy aimed at making everyone hate him- or herself deeply while also feeling as though books are improving his or her life and intellect. The mainstream media has propagandized books into coveted, lofty items, and people have agreed without listening to their own feelings or inner voices screaming: *NO! Books hurt! They're too hard to understand and I want to play Wii!* Many misconceptions about reading have permeated our culture. I will now debunk several of these myths:

Misconception 1: Reading Makes You Smarter

One reason to own books is that some people believe having more books around the house results in smarter, more successful children, even if said children never open the books themselves.[7] That means people who are out buying up books left and right might not read at all. Even people who supposedly love reading, those who make language their "calling," do the bare minimum of required reading. Did you

---

6. Little known fact: Early editions of the *Federalist Papers* were designed this way to trick John Adams into looking at them.

7. This was from *Freakonomics*. It's the book that shows several correlations between being alive and being a terrible person.

know that college students spend less than 7 percent of their time at school studying? It's their "job" to read books, and they still only spend 7 percent of their time doing it. The other 93 percent of their time is spent drunkenly explaining why Chuck Palahniuk is "like, the greatest writer of our time, but I can't really articulate why right now."[8] Somehow, though, a bunch of people decided that reading was the only thing that makes you smarter.

Those people are wrong. Instead, holding or owning books only makes you seem smarter, but everyone could seem smarter by wearing a suit and practicing refined public speaking habits.[9] You can also seem smarter by carrying books around everywhere. Sometimes I'll spend an hour perusing titles at a bookstore, then finally choose the one with the most interesting cover art and carry it around another bookstore until someone asks me about it.[10]

You may be surprised to discover that many great thinkers hated reading. Francis Bacon literally consumed books, saying: "Some books are to be tasted, others to be swallowed, and some few to be chewed and digested."[11] Einstein, also arguably one of the smartest men in history, said (and I'm paraphrasing here): "Reading is for pussies." Are you a pussy? Do you want a nerd like Einstein calling you a pussy? I didn't think so. Ezra Pound, attempting to convince others of the benefits of

---

8. A statistic that should have been in *Freakonomics* since drunk people who can't remember their point are the most terrible.

9. Barack Obama hasn't read a thing since 2008. That's why he wrote that picture book.

10. Even if that person is a security guard asking if I stole the book, I feel that carrying around the book has earned me some much-needed human attention.

11. For the record, I did not read this quote in a book but heard it spoken by Leonard Nimoy while playing the video game Civilization IV. It's like Risk only more racist and historically inaccurate.

books, said, "A book should be a ball of light in one's hands." He then picked a random book from his library shelf, held it at arm's length, and yelled "Hadouken!" Nothing happened. He then recanted, saying: "I said a book 'should be.' It should be able to become a blue ball of fire that defeats my opponent in battle."[12]

Some believe that when you do open books and actually read them, you'll be more intelligent because you will have more thoughts and facts inside your brain. Another case for the dumbness of reading, however, is that books do not contain answers, but rather pose more questions. And asking questions makes you look dumber, not smarter. I thought *Alice's Adventures in Wonderland* would be a delightful romp through a child's subconscious, but while reading that children's novel I started to ask questions like "How do you really speak to other humans when our language often means the opposite of what is intended?" and "How do I really know anyone?" And so on, until I was asking the question "Why even exist at all?" That didn't make me smarter! That made me wish for death, and being dead looks way dumber than being alive.

Because books lead to more questions about reality, readers often sound like they're still sorting everything out in their heads. What uncharismatic wimps! Be a man and pretend to know everything! If you'd like to look smarter, tell everyone a philosophy you came up with in sixth grade and never expanded further through reading. People will love how confident you sound.[13]

---

12. For older readers (nay, less lonely readers), "Hadouken" refers to a special move in the Street Fighter games. Ezra Pound loved Street Fighter so much he wrote a few Cantos about how many cheap moves Blanka and E. Honda were capable of. See also *The Electric Hundred Hand Slap Cantos*.

13. One annoying example: "Everything in moderation . . . especially moderation." Yuck. I just threw up a little while writing that.

Misconception 2: Reading Is a Great Leisure Activity

Most people don't have time to read, but in their minds the perfect day features some "great" novel or other: sunning in a hammock, listening to the sound of crickets, and reading *One Hundred Years of Solitude*.

These people are misguided. Reading is the only leisurely activity that feels like work.[14] Every time I read more than twenty pages, my neck hurts, my vision is blurred, and I somehow always let my mind wander to thoughts about eating or pooping.[15] How can we stay focused when it takes several of these painful twenty-minute chunks to finish children's books like *The Hunger Games* and everything Glenn Beck ever wrote?

In reality, there are only a few ways to make reading tolerable. Nothing will ever make it fun, but you can find ways to entertain yourself. Whenever I read, I like to pretend comedian Sam Kinison is yelling all the words at me.[16] I also pace the floor while reading. While pacing, I like to write a few notes in the margins about how I'm feeling that have nothing to do with the book. Then, I like to feed my dog, make a grocery list, play Tetris while listening to a book on tape, and then check my email while reading the book on an iPad. I also like to take mushrooms and stare at the book's cover for an hour or so until it turns into the ocean, then I step into that ocean of words and swim around until

---

14. Unless you count trying to understand any David Lynch movie. ZING!!!

15. I wrote this sentence while pooping . . . and eating . . .

16. "It's A TRUTH! A UNIVERSALLY ACKNOWLEDGED FUCKING TRUTH *GODDAMNIT*, THAT A MAN . . . A STUPID RICH COCKSUCKER WHO FINALLY FOUND A FORTUNE . . . will be in want of a wife. And that wife will end up becoming A BLOOD-SUCKING WHOOOOORRE!—Sam Kinison reading Jane Austen's *Pride and Prejudice*.

I no longer feel I have a self but rather that I'm part of a greater word-world that we could all join if we just looked through the correct set of eyes.[17] All of the strategies listed here, however, are more fun when you subtract the book: imitating Sam Kinison, video games, doing drugs.

Misconception 3: Reading Connects You to Others

Many people think reading will help them understand the people around them better, and help them live more emotionally fulfilling lives. These people are wrong. Reading helps people ignore everything except the words on the paper. A terrible way to make friends is by meeting them at a coffee shop, then pulling out some strange device that requires all your attention. If you want to make friends, just drink more and hang out in places where people talk. How many friends have you met while legitimately studying in a library? None. But if you stop reading and ask a girl if that book's any good, she'll gladly stop reading and flirt because reading is loathsome.

For those of you who don't know, reading is like TV without all the pictures. It's another passive activity that, unlike video games and social media, severs you from all human contact. Unlike movies, you can't share a book on a first date.[18] Plus, reading is best done in solitude and silence. Books are basically math problems, only lonelier since even telepathic aliens who communicate using mathematics won't be able to relate to the "joys" of reading books. They'll listen to your unsophisticated and arcane word-thoughts, then enslave you.

---

17. Wow! Maybe it's just the drugs talking, but books are awesome when you don't read them! Excuse me, gotta poop again!

18. Although, a twenty-hour date where you both read *Unbearable Lightness of Being* will have a fun ending. (It's about fucking.)

Reading to get closer to others is hopeless, especially when, as is often the case, you decide to never finish reading the recommended book. Now you've tried to relate to someone through text, and you're more alone than ever because you couldn't finish. Besides, no book will ever help you get through a conversation as well as ruminating on why a TV show you both loved was unfairly canceled.[19]

Exchanging books is even trickier territory. Giving someone a book is like saying, "Here: take this and never give it back. You could get this book at any library and keep it well past the return date, but instead of late fees, I'd like you to pay me in shame dollars and friendship points. I'm going to hang this over your head for the rest of our lives even though I'd never open that book again if it remained in my house." That's no way to become friends with someone. Ask that person instead for a family heirloom or a cat. You could even steal either of these things. Then the person will go out of his or her way to contact you more often!

Why I Hate Reading: My Story

In grade school I was subject to the harsh yolk of Sustained Silent Reading Time, which, they could have just called "reading time," but I guess they wanted kids to feel awful and learn what the word "sustained" means.[20] Once, the entire school had Sustained Silent Reading Time in the gym because the best place to cuddle up with a good book is on

---

19. *Arrested Development* could have gone so far!" is the only statement you have to remember on a first date with anyone worth sleeping with. *Firefly too.*

20. It means "terrible," right?

hardwood floors while sitting knee to knee with smelly fifth graders. I suffered from a common condition called Chubby Legs, and as we read for nearly an hour, my stumps were deprived of the already-poor circulation they so desperately needed. I tried to stretch a bit but ended up kicking the student in front of me. I apologized and heard the hiss of my teacher whispering: "Daniel, come here this instant." My legs were asleep at this point, and the moment I put weight on them, my knees buckled and I was suddenly crowd surfing over three hundred groggy eleven-year-olds who, all at the same moment, gave up reading for the day. Reading had made me the laughingstock of the school, but by becoming a distraction I had freed friends (if only for a moment) from the tyranny of books.

After grade school and high school, I braved the frightful waters of academia, and came out a broken, beaten burnout, all because I succeeded (though I would not call this feat a success) in reading not just one book, but several books, written before 1901. I know! It's shocking to think anyone would even fathom reaching back that far into the garble of barbarism, but I held my head up high, put my nose to the proverbial ink ribbon, and received an F on three or four papers in a row.[21]

At the risk of losing your trust, I will inform you that during this time, I also read a few good books from the past century ("Fire of my

21. A few papers were awful because I wasted time reading the text (I'm talking to you, *Daniel Deronda*!) instead of forcing myself to get a head start on finishing the papers. Let it be known: I endorse starting papers before you finish books in college. I'm serious. You need sleep. If you're in college reading this book, stop reading, and start your stupid paper. Seriously. At least open a blank document on the computer and put your name and date on it! Start it now, you lazy schmuck! Just a genuine tip for anyone in school. And now on to the rest of this book!

loins," "So it goes," etc.[22]). I confess that nearly three of the pages I consumed meant something deeper than I'd expected.[23] But while skimming chapter after chapter of these diatribes, I found myself thinking: *Get to the point!* So what if your main character eats, breathes, has sex like the rest of us? WE WANT THE MEAT OF THE STORY! Don't give us this reflective-of-the-times subplot where one character drones on about architecture! You're making reading worse than it already is!

I should have given up on books way back in grade school. But it wasn't until June 2, 2010—the day a book killed my father—that I finally turned my back on reading for good. See Appendix C.

Pie Chart: What Really Matters

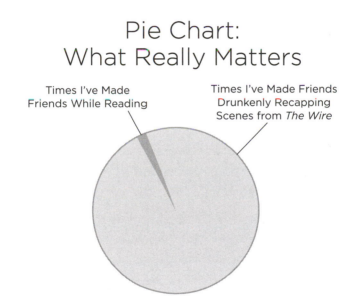

Times I've Made Friends While Reading

Times I've Made Friends Drunkenly Recapping Scenes from *The Wire*

---

22. *Lolita* and *Slaughterhouse-Five*, just in case you're trying to look smart in front of people who claim they read a lot. Cool people love these books!

23. Last page of *Rabbit at Rest*; two pages in *Where's Waldo?*

QUICK TIPS FOR LOOKING SMARTER RIGHT AWAY

Like all good manual writers, I know that you will probably never read this book from cover to cover, so, for those of you who wish to be better at chess by skimming the back cover of a chess book, or those who want to start a pond in the backyard after reading one article online, here are some quick tips that will help you stop reading this book and get to work on your new life/Sunday afternoon:

Buy used books: They're cheap, and someone already did the work of bending the spines and underlining smart quotes. Open it up, read a random line. Start claiming you've read it!

Write elaborate fake inscriptions: If someone takes a book off your shelf and reads the title page, now he or she is not asking what you've been reading lately, but instead "Who's Denise? She sounds really into you!" Better yet, write a few from celebrities. No one too famous, but just famous enough that it's a possibility he or she gave you a book (e.g., "To Dan, from one avid reader to another, Wesley Snipes").

Play Scrabble on your Kindle: It will seem like you're taking copious notes, but really you just beat a computer at your favorite word game. Who's in charge now, Skynet?!

Read the back or inside flap description: This might seem obvious if you've ever written a book report in grade school but 50 percent of the time, you can still pass as well-read by regurgitating a few words of copy! Easy things to remember: "I found the portrayal of the character's occupation thrilling and well researched. A must-read!"

Quick research on Wikipedia: Think of a movie you enjoy. If that movie is based on a novel, learn EXACTLY ONE PART the screenwriter changed for the film version. Bring that up in every conversation about that book (e.g., Did you ever read *Dune*? The movie missed SO MUCH!").

Look at the cover/title: Judge accordingly.

CHAPTER ONE

Books

What Are They, and What Are They Good For?

You've probably heard of books before. Perhaps a movie star or pro athlete recently indicted for drug possession appeared on a poster informing you to read books if you'd like to become better at acting or drug using. If you didn't realize yet, you're holding a book right now! Don't you love the feel of the pages? The smell, the look, the physical weight of so many thoughts waiting to be absorbed in pure intellectual bliss?[1]

What is a book? The Merriam-Webster definition of a book is: pages bound (bound to make me sleepy, AMIRIGHT?![2]) together by glue or

---

1. Or, if you're looking at this on an e-reader: Don't you love the . . . words? How they . . . appear on an Etch A Sketch–looking screen and how you can access Wikipedia whenever you want? Or how warm the battery feels as it slowly gives you ball cancer?

2. I apologize.

leather or something. If you're reading a single sheet of paper above the sink telling you to "please clean your own dishes," that's a note, and should not be brought up in book clubs or classes, since others do not count notes as high literature.[3] If many pieces of paper are stapled or folded together, then it's a pamphlet. Pamphlets can be useful: Karl Marx wrote a pamphlet. Pamphlets stop STDs (or rather, inform readers where and how they can contract one after they've already caught it).

Yet, compared to other types of media, books play a less exciting yet ironically more prestigious role in society. On a scale of one to smart, books are number one! Even self-published books (Merriam-Webster definition: any book that is so bad not even its author wants to read it) are thought to be higher on the intellectual food chain than other pieces of media. Here are the other media you may know about and that aren't considered to be as prestigious as books:

- Cable news, which tells you what to think
- Magazines, which are pamphlets that tell you your body is gross
- Music, which tells you about sex through Auto-Tune
- Newspapers, which are nearly as boring as books except they can be easily used to make papier-mâché art and funny hats
- Radio, like NPR, which keeps you informed about the migration habits of extinct birds while constantly asking you for money
- Personal blogs, which remind people of movies they used to like by posting stills from those movies
- News blogs, which tell people extremely important information if they can resist the urge to click on the recently released celebrity sex tape right next to that important information

---

3. Unless you're an aspiring poet who reads William Carlos Williams, in which case, anything goes, I guess.

- Theater, which helps people remember that guy from that one episode of that show
- TV, which uses product placement to force you to buy stuff like a delicious KFC Double Down or a refreshing Heineken
- Movies, which are closest to narrative books, except in a movie you know a character is evil if he is shown cheating on his wife, whereas in a book, the guy cheating on his wife is the hero.[4]

Books are the medium able to explore the inner workings of the mind, share scientific and historical facts, and examine our collective emotional experience, but they are mostly used as a way for washed-up famous people to get a second wind.

Is This Thing I'm Holding a Book?

If you think you may be reading a book, here are some features to look out for:

- A cover that is thicker than the inside pages
- Titles in classy fonts
- A page number on the bottom corner of each page so you can see your progress
- The title or the author's name on the top of each page so you don't suddenly forget what you're reading
- Long blurbs from semifamous people, one-word blurbs from very famous people

---

4. See most fiction, including *The Odyssey*.

- Author photo on last page: flattering but not very sexy, unless the author received a book deal solely on his or her looks.[5]

What Else Might I Be Holding?

If you see some of these features but still do not think you're holding a book, the object might be a small gaming system like a Nintendo DS. Occasionally, video games feature writing. Be not afraid! Video games can be fun without reading. Much like a fantasy novel, if you're bored with a video game's story line, you can skip all the dialogue and go right to the action sequences.[6]

You might also be holding your cell phone. Phones also have pictures and text-based information. The difference between a phone and a book, however, is that a phone is something you ignore when your parents are trying to contact you, whereas books can be ignored for nearly any reason.

Is Reading Books Good for Me?

Many people think reading is a healthy activity because they have never read a book. In reality, reading is sedentary and lonely. Childhood obe-

---

5. Like this book. Right, *laaaaaadiiesssss*?

6. Fantasy novels also feature fake maps of fake worlds at the beginning, making fantasy novels slightly less fun than a video game. Fantasy novels are more like a video game strategy guide.

sity is at an all-time high, and one of our solutions is forcing kids to sit inside and stare at books all day instead of exercising outside by playing "ding dong ditch" or running from the house they just vandalized. Many fear their children have gone off the deep end with video games, and think their kids should spend more time sitting in the same spot on the couch, reading. Reading in the same room as a video game system, however, is like sitting next to someone screaming, "STOP READING!"

However, reading isn't entirely negative. Most of what an adolescent learns from books is filtered through a brain forcing itself *not* to do something more fun than reading. This is healthy. The only way to teach children that they can't do whatever they want whenever they want is by robbing them of their youth and forcing them to read instead of enjoying themselves. This habit will teach kids to ignore their impulses while pretending to enjoy an activity that is objectively dreadful. The ability to feign enjoyment will prove useful while watching their peers (or even, one day, their own children) perform theater.

OTHER EVILS BOOKS ARE RESPONSIBLE FOR

- John Lennon's murder (inspired by *The Catcher in the Rye*)
- Competitive beard growing (Hemingway's fault)
- Killing trees, since most books are made of paper
- The spread of bedbugs (books are their favorite space!)
- 90 percent of paper cuts
- Organized religion
- Your aunt's constant insistence that she's "turning over a new leaf" (caused by most self-help books)
- A book was seen on the grassy knoll the day JFK was shot.

Books can also be a great resource for feeding your mind ambitious future writer or critic thoughts like "I could have written this book" and "This book sucks."

Reading is also a healthy escape from the real world. Unlike radio and TV, which you can talk over or ignore for a moment or two, books require one voice to overpower all the other voices inside your crowded brain. The only way to enjoy a book is to suppress your own thoughts, a great escape from the dramas of the real world and the dramas between your multiple personalities.

Another reason to read books is that stories provide a bit of excitement in an otherwise humdrum existence. Though TV and human speech can relate stories more vibrantly than books, televisions and friends rarely enter the home of a self-proclaimed "reader." Reading is about as interesting as loading a dishwasher, but to people who only spend their "fun time" after work loading their dishwasher, reading appears to be a great journey through time and space (really, it's sitting alone and making yourself more alone by not even trying to leave the house).

The important fact to remember is that while there are a few good side effects of reading, few people actually read. Instead, everyone likes pretending they read. If we spent as much time reading as we say we do, we'd be grossly overweight and depressed.

What Else Are Books Good For?

If you never plan on reading another book for the rest of your life, there are other great uses for them:

- Storing a rock hammer to escape Shawshank Prison
- For kindling after a horrific plane crash that leaves a few survivors

forced to cook and eat frozen bodies (Good thing someone bought that Tom Clancy book just before takeoff!)

- Tearing the introductory pages out to teach students how poetry should really be related: by screaming "O Captain! My Captain!" while standing on your desk
- Forcing someone not to lie in a courtroom by making that person touch the book (Certain frightening books actually have this power!)

Another great use for books is as gifts to a friend for a birthday or graduation. Be wary, though, books are the hardest gift to feign excitement about. The receiver of the gift will most likely say, "Thank you. This means so much!" then get back to you about reading the book five months later, if ever.

However, if you do choose to give a book as a gift, here are a few suggestions to get you started:

GREAT GIFT IDEAS

Everyone Poops (for a child or an adult you suspect might not know this information)

What to Expect When You're Expecting (Only for women you know are pregnant! DO NOT GUESS!)

The Seven Habits of Highly Effective People (All you have to do is own it in order to become a success! 15 million copies sold = 15 million famous success stories)

Stay away from the following:

BAD GIFT IDEAS

Any of the *You on a Diet* books (You will get slapped, especially if you give it to a woman who is, or you thought was, pregnant.)

Lolita to a high school girl, while winking (possible jail time)

Heaven Is for Real (It's not. Don't confuse people.)

The Seven Habits of High People (Not as good as the other book with a similar title; mostly just paranoid people talking about how awesome Jean-Claude Van Damme movies are.)

WHAT HAVE I BEEN DOING BESIDES READING?

The omnipresence of books might lead you to think that people are reading all the time. Though reading seems very popular, often daily routines and other forms of entertainment get in the way. If you don't read books and are wondering why you don't, here is a brief list of other activities that have distracted many people from reading:

Waking up

Getting out of bed

Eating breakfast

Checking Facebook

Getting on the train to go to work

Talking to coworkers

Looking at photos on Facebook

Avoiding your boss at work

Walking around the office

Stapling things at your desk to look busy

Picking lint from your belly button

Going to the gym

Returning to work

Eating your lunch

Leaving the office early

Staring at women on the subway

Staring at art

Staring at a wall

Spending time with your family

Pizza (it's so good!)

Television (this goes great with pizza!)

Drinking (goes great with pizza and TV)

Looking at more Facebook photos

Drinking more than is considered healthy

Facebook stalking ex-girlfriends

Drinking even more

Getting caught by wife sending messages to ex-girlfriends

Signing a separation agreement

Drinking while you're supposed to be reading said agreement

Drinking and driving

Drinking and driving while checking Facebook

Drinking and driving to your ex-girlfriend's house

Drinking and getting the door slammed in your face

Drinking and driving in a school zone

Getting caught by the police while drunkenly doing donuts in a school
parking lot when you thought the school was closed (even if it was,
you can still get arrested)

Finding a lawyer on Google

Calling another lawyer after finding out that one only specialized in child
custody disputes

Noting to keep that lawyer's number for when you have to get your kids
back

Pleading no contest

Losing your kids

Calling the other lawyer after all

Failing to get kids back

Microwaving a bowl of Campbell's tomato soup

Burning yourself after not waiting long enough for soup to cool

Running cold water over burned appendages

Swearing

Vomiting

Drinking after vomiting

Walking to same school that caused you to lose everything

Remembering the good old days when that school seemed so large

Remembering your teachers

Ruminating on how old your hot preschool teacher, Ms. Pruxley, must be

Wondering what she's up to now, at age fifty-three

Facebook-stalking Ms. Pruxley

Deciding by the looks of Ms. Pruxley's Facebook profile that it "could go either way"

Calling her

Meeting up for drinks at Applebee's

Realizing she's going through nearly the same shit you are

Asking Ms. Pruxley to come home with you too suddenly

Realizing your mistake

Going home alone

Stalking your ex-wife on Facebook

Drinking and riding your bike to blow off steam

Explaining to a cop that you had no idea drunk bike riding could land you a DUI

Ruminating on this terrible law for hours in a jail cell, as it is your second offense

Calling ex-wife

Crying and crying and crying and crying

Getting released from jail, being told to never do anything like this again

Trying meth with Ms. Pruxley

Starting to make meth in your bathtub

Finding out from other dealers how not to die while making meth in your bathtub

Slowly running out of meth

Turning to prostitution to afford ingredients

Pimping Ms. Pruxley[7]

Reading more on cheaper ways to make meth

Realizing how cool meth is

Watching a lot of *Breaking Bad*

Realizing people might enjoy your memoir

Writing entire book during meth-rage fever

Submitting memoir to Penguin

Getting advance

Spending advance on DirecTV

Updating Facebook

Dying in sleep at age fifty-nine

---

7. The title of my next book! *Am I right?!?!?*

CHAPTER TWO

A Brief History of Books

Who Were the First Readers and Writers?

The first reader was born into the world of an entirely different artistic vision. The son of an Irish actor and mathematics professor, he spent time as a child training as an actor himself. Since he grew up around several siblings also training to be actors, he retreated to his room and brooded as if constantly reading. Up to this point, many middle-class families owned books for the purposes of decoration, but no one had finished reading one. Envy and sibling rivalry gave way to actual study, and soon the young actor moved from scripts to real books without telling anyone but his father. "Surely, this 'reading' thing is purely teenage rebellion," the father told his wife, while secretly wondering if his son had actually read a book, something he had tried many times but failed to do. After an awkward talk from his father about the merits of not reading in school, the son went off to college and, in an attempt to conceal his love of books from his professors, doubled down and quit before the end of his first year to pursue acting. He starred in several movies as a teenage underdog and outsider (the way he'd often felt at home) and was fawned over by many female fans. But he never let the public know he had read an entire book until much later.

This man? John Cusack.

Cusack came out to the world about his book fetish when he produced a cinematic adaptation of Nick Hornby's *High Fidelity*. Though Hornby wrote several novels and essays, the first to ever be read by another human was *High Fidelity*. Cusack, knowing no one would ever watch some smarty-pants British guy rant about books and music, cleverly placed the main character in Chicago, a city where everyone pretends to read but not so much so that they sound like stuck-up assholes.[1] Cusack also cast himself as the main character, revealing a groundbreaking way to enjoy books: pretending to be the main character. This idea changed reading culture for years to come (that is to say, it changed the lives of nearly two hundred thousand people). What a great moment in literary history! To this day, however, no other person has read *High Fidelity*, including Nick Hornby's editor.[2] Before Cusack made this movie, many movies were based on books, but for the most part, movie studios bought the rights to the book's title and simply guessed what the plot of the book was.

Since the beginning of reading books (1995), many have forced reading on other people as a form of adolescent corporal punishment. Though the history of reading is very short (it started with Cusack and the trend will certainly be phased out before his death), the history of writing and books is much longer. New readers have retrieved myriad information concerning how reading and writing came to be, and after

---

1. If you're wondering if I'm talking about your city, you're right. It's you.

2. Cusack continued to shove his love for books in the public's face by starring in the movie *2012*, where he played a popular writer of books. What a show-off!

years of study and scholarly discussion, sociologists and American Studies majors agree: Books exist. But how exactly did they come to exist?

Writing Up to Now: A Brief Review of Its History and the Western Canon

If you take a second to think about how many books exist, and how rarely people read, you realize how wrong it is to waste that much paper and energy. I would like to condense for you the history of writing and books in order to save humans valuable time and resources that they would otherwise spend on even longer books about the following subjects. Hopefully, you will be able to relate these summations to friends with even fewer words, rather than following this needless trend to write longer books about other books.[3] So now a quick rundown of everything that came before the Great Cusack Breakthrough of 1995.

Hunter-Gatherer Cave Painters

Early nomadic humans were forced to follow and kill beasts in the field. Those who could not hunt, however, drew pictures of hunting on cave walls. The bigger cavemen counted this as a skill, and let these painters live. Eventually, sons of cavemen were born who were able to hunt but

---

3. Then those friends can make those summaries even shorter, until, generations from now, we will be able to simply wink and everyone will know the winker is referencing Kant's categorical imperative.

felt like painting instead. This led to many cave-fathers saying things like "No son of Grogdor is going to sit in the cave all day looking at pictures! To the fields you go!" This only made the expressive youths more determined to create "little stories" of hunting out in the field, distracting others who were hunting real animals. This became the first form of theater, which cave-fathers agreed was "way worse" than anything their odd sons had done so far. When these boys would return home, they would speak at length around the fire about how important stories were, until their dads disowned them. Those first storytellers who survived did so by estranging themselves from their fathers and families. This is why most great literature involves weird daddy issues.

What they wrote: All that is left from this era of storytelling is paintings of buffalo.

Famous quote: "Buffalo buffalo Buffalo buffalo buffalo buffalo Buffalo buffalo." (This is not the famous grammar puzzle, but a story with a beginning, middle, and end that roughly translates to "There a buffalo; there buffalo too." Most writing before the invention of verbs is difficult to understand.)

Cuneiform Writers

Cuneiform was the very first writing that featured symbols instead of pictures. This alphabet led to more and more abstract representations of objects, until people were asking profound questions like "What is this thing?" and others were answering with words instead of grunt noises, or drawing a picture of the thing and saying, "This . . . This is that thing" (which wasn't very helpful).

What they wrote: *Gilgamesh*, an epic featuring early versions of Noah's Ark and the fall of Man, dismissed by most later religions as juvenile and "not as good as the Bible." Though not a piece of Western literature, it is often read by Western students when they're given a choice to read *Gilgamesh* instead of several longer epics.[4] The story follows a king who is given a natural-man best friend by the gods, who then arbitrarily kill the man once the king becomes emotionally attached. So the moral of the first story in recorded history is "If you love someone, that person will die for no good reason." Wow. If stories are meant to depress people, then human beings knocked it out of the park on their first try.

Famous quote: "Why should I not wander over the pastures in search of the wind?" Here is yet another indication that reading or writing does not necessarily make you smarter: The first story featured a guy chasing wind.

Egyptians

Egyptians drew pictures that represented words rather than symbols that represented words. Apparently they didn't get the memo that people were past picture-words, probably because that memo was written in Cuneiform.

What they wrote: stories about pharaohs being the best because they were pharaohs. Also *The Book of the Dead*, a manual of what to say at someone's funeral, because people were tired of hearing super-awkward eulogies like "This Pharaoh was great. He loved it when I fanned him with enormous leaves . . . uhhh . . . Well, that's all I really know about him."

Famous quote: "Bird, Ankh, Different Bird, Ankh, Ankh, Bird." (Trans: "Do unto others whatever the hell you feel like. You're the pharaoh, baby! Now, go out and enslave some Jews!")

---

4. *The Iliad*? Six hundred pages. *Gilgamesh*? Fifty pages. Graduating from college with a Classics degree after reading for one hour? Priceless.

The Jews

The Jewish people are still around today (though not for lack of trying on the part of people who wanted them dead). The Jews started as a tribe in Israel and survived slavery, exile in a desert, and genocide. They are the first writers to prove that terrible experiences often lead to decent literature.

What they wrote: stories about pharaohs being huge assholes because they were pharaohs. They also wrote rules on large rock slabs to stop devastating wars, personal disputes, and wasting time worshipping the wrong god. They eventually caused devastating wars, personal disputes, and the worship of the most famous wrong god, Jesus Christ.

Famous quote: "I am the Lord, Your God, who took you out of the house of bondage." Although most people were happy about this, many who enjoyed bondage were annoyed. Before that, the bondage-lovers were pleased to find Sodom and Gomorrah, but God stepped all over that fun time, too.[5]

Homer

Homer was a sea-savvy bard who produced the greatest stories and poems in human history. Usually taught to eighth graders by screening film versions.

What he wrote: *The Odyssey* and *The Iliad*—long poems about the adventures of manly men doing manly things like fighting wars, assaulting cave monsters, and having sex with other men. The moral of *The Odyssey* is "If you come home to find one hundred dudes flirting

---

5. Interesting fact: Most Jewish tribes used "Yahweh" as a safe word during sex, hence the strict rules about throwing the name around willy-nilly.

with your wife, you should count backward from ten before killing everyone and starting a civil war." The moral of *The Iliad* is "Never kill the invincible dude's boyfriend."

Famous quote: "Hateful to me as the gates of Hades is that man who hides one thing in his heart but says another." Achilles says this in Homer's *Illiad*, while trying to get everyone to give him an honest opinion about whether or not his Cuirass made him look fat.

Greek Tragedians: Aeschylus, Euripides, Sophocles

Because the Athenians were trapped between some mountains and no other countries could see them, they were able to play dress-up and have adult pretend time without being (rightfully) mocked. They also felt the need to entertain themselves without putting all their hateful intellectuals to death. Though humans are a renewable resource and fun to kill, the Greeks wanted to see death more often than they had citizens to murder, so they hired people to act out fake deaths: deaths that became stranger and more frightening as the years progressed.

What they wrote: Each wrote lyric plays about people murdering everyone in their families for complicated reasons. Each play was performed one time, in front of everyone in Athens.[6]

The Oresteia, a trilogy by Aeschylus, was also known as *Wait Till Your Father Gets Home . . . Because My New Lover and I Are Going to Stab Him to Death*.

Euripides' *Medea* was originally titled *Honey I Shrunk the Kids . . . into Small Pieces of Dead Bodies Because You Betrayed Me!*

Sophocles wrote *Oedipus Rex*, which was a cautionary tale about

---

6. Interesting fact: None of the plays included stage directions, because actors were supposed to dodge the audience's drunken vomit streams and errant punches.

fixing the Grecian adoption process. It also perpetuated the old wives' tale "If you screw your mom too much, you'll go blind."

Famous quote: "A human being is only breath and shadow." From Sophocles, while advertising his new fragrance for men, Breath&Shadow.

Aristophanes, Greek Comic Playwright

Aristophanes wrote elaborate satirical plays about people trying to make a new home in the clouds and plays about how much school sucks. Aristophanes' plays have the best of dick jokes: "Hey, everyone. You ever wonder what a Cyclops penis looks like? I bet it has two eyes, right?! Don't get me started on the Hydra! HAHA! MORE WINE! MORE, I SAY!"

What he wrote: *Lysistrata*, a play about women refusing sex until the men ended a war. Same strategy is used today in war over how late men are permitted to stay out drinking with their friends. Aristophanes also wrote several plays making fun of real-life Athenian politicians and scholars, including *The Wasps*, where one character says, "How about this latest sex scandal with Cleon, huh? I mean I understand cheating on your wife: Heterosexual love is disgusting! But at least wait until the boy is seven years old! Younger than that and it's gross!" Greece had a very different view of sexual morality.

Famous quote: "Characteristics of a popular politician: a horrible voice, bad breeding, and a vulgar manner." Most people who could vote in Athens were considered politicians, so Aristophanes was alienating everyone in town.

Herodotus

Herodotus wrote history the way it should be written: no facts, with made-up gods behind any historical moment that defies explanation.

What he wrote: *The Histories*, a lengthy account of the Persians fighting the Greeks, the causes of which are obvious to anyone who studies history: Zeus and some other gods decided it should be that way.

Famous quote: "Illness strikes men when they are exposed to change." He then added, ". . . and by change, I mean syphilis."

Thucydides

Thucydides was the failure who tried to write history using empirical data and first-person accounts of a war. What an idiot!

What he wrote: *The History of the Peloponnesian War.* The book covers how everyone in Athens fucked himself by constantly voting on ways to destroy other countries with an already overextended military. Voters veered toward "Death to all!" but occasionally slaughtered only the adult males. Those were some thoughtful citizens!

Famous quote: "He who graduates the harshest school, succeeds." Thucydides said this at the grand opening of his private school, A-Punch-to-the-Nuts-Until-You-Learn-All-Greek-Noun-Declensions School for Boys.

Hippocrates

Hippocrates was the first doctor to actually help people feel better and live longer rather than just open up people's bodies to see what was inside. The unforeseen innovation of using people's bodies for something other than freakish sexual experimentation helped many Greeks survive deadly diseases like ankle sprains and bleeding from the finger.

What he wrote: A treatise on how to *not* kill people. Up to that point, there wasn't even a Greek word for "aid" or "revive"; there was only *anamorire a sancca*, which roughly translates: "To a man, in his cups: I killed him slower for my own sake!"[7]

Famous quote: (while wiggling finger) "If it hurts when you do this . . . don't do this anymore!"[8]

Plato

Plato wrote down everything his teacher, Socrates, said. What a suck-up! Plato also wrote many famous dialogues showing students how easy it is to ruin another person's argument by asking more questions. Example: "Why are you so stupid? Does your mother know you're stupid?"

What he wrote: *The Republic*, defining a perfect city as one with great lakefront developments and several four-star restaurants. Also he wrote *The Symposium*, which featured many drunk people claiming different genders were once physically attached to each other, and *The Apology of Socrates*, in which Socrates says he does not fear death for it's either a large party with famous fictional characters or it's like a really good nap. All of these writings are further evidence that marijuana was available in Athens.

Famous quote: From *The Apology*: "Socrates said: 'I knew I was smarter than others because I knew that which I did not know.'" Many think Socrates was saying that he was wise for knowing his own ignorance, but he was really saying that he knew more than everyone save for a few people who knew how to crochet, which he wanted to learn before his death.

---

7. Most Greek adages translate to something like this.

8. The first doctor also wrote the very first one-liner about being a doctor. No one laughed, yet doctors continue to tell terrible jokes even today!

Aristotle

Aristotle was the first writer to take a guess at what physics was all about. The results he came up with were: Some rocks are harder than other rocks and only five elements make up the universe: earth, wind, water, fire, and ether.[9] Aristotle taught these facts to many students, including Alexander the Great, who was the first person to prove that a good education can turn you into a huge asshole.

What he wrote: Among other things, *Poetics*, a guide to writing plays. Aristotle invented the inciting incident and the gay character for comic relief in a rom-com.

Famous quote: From *Poetics*: "Poetry in hexameter is as good an entertainment as man will ever know. I mean, unless they make a magic box where you can actually see Odysseus sailing around—BAH! The thought alone makes me laugh. Hexameter. Number one. Forever."

Euclid

Euclid was responsible for mathematical axioms still used today, and therefore responsible for your weak SAT scores keeping you out of the Ivy League. Your two minutes of hate may be directed at Euclid.

What he wrote: *Elements*, a reference tool for answering heretofore unanswerable questions about geometry, like "What is the fastest way from point A to point B?" Many pre-Math smart-asses answered "running." Euclid's answer was less funny. Geometry also taught people how to cut up pizza evenly.

Famous quote: "The Laws of Nature are mathematical thoughts of

---

9. Aristotle is responsible for the children's TV series *Captain Planet*, but the creators changed the last element from ether to "heart" because they were all on ether.

[handwritten annotation: ↶ Like this?]

God." If you look at a parabola the right way, it seems to be one of God's dirtier thoughts.

Archimedes

Archimedes was an astronomer, inventor, engineer, and mathematician. To be fair, though, in order to be specialized in any discipline during the Greek Empire, all you had to do was drink with the right group of guys and say one sentence about each subject. Archimedes' principle that "if you stare at shapes long enough, you can see some patterns" made him the most famous math guy. Archimedes was killed by a Roman soldier during a siege of Syracuse, because he would not look up from a math problem he was intent on finishing. Sadly, that math problem was one his friend posed: "If you have a pound of feathers and a pound of rocks, which weighs more?" Poor Archimedes sat for hours trying to figure it out! He never solved this clever riddle. Unless he's in Heaven solving it now.[10]

[handwritten annotation: overwritten manuscript]

What he wrote: *The Archimedes' Palimpsest,* which describes how to measure a circle and how to build super-sweet ship-destroying war machines, proving that math is sometimes badass.

Famous quote: While bathing, Archimedes devised a way to prove a goldsmith had ripped off King Hiero and shouted from his bathtub, "Eureka!" (literally "I have found it") before running naked down the street. The naked Archimedes had a way to prove that the goldsmith had stolen from the king, and he shouted, "Finally, I can convince the king to kill that thieving bastard! O, Archimedes! You will get blood on your hands yet! WEEE!!!! PUBLIC EXECUTION DAAAAAAYYYY!!!"

---

10. He's not.

If you spend too much time studying math, you get an insatiable thirst for blood.

Virgil

Virgil wrote an epic poem about the founding of Rome by the most pious of men, Aeneas, which made perfect sense since Rome was a decadent balls-out fuck-party every day of the year.[11]

What he wrote: *The Aeneid*. He told his friends while on his deathbed to burn it. It's thought to be one of the finest works of literature, so think for a second about how good you think your poetry is, then realize Virgil thought his best work was awful. Yours is probably *really* shitty.

Famous quote: "Fortune favors the bold." Virgil had all his poems printed in boldface type, which improved sales greatly.

New Testament Writers

The writers of the New Testament wrote down everything Jesus ever said or did, only they weren't there to actually hear or see any of it, so people nowadays take it with a big grain of salt (right?). Most of the

---

11. Aeneas roamed much of the world before founding Italy. One of his adventures led to accidentally tricking Dido, a queen, into thinking she and Aeneas were married before having sex with her in a cave and slipping off in the early morning to sail away. This was the first ever one-night stand on record, and Dido did not take it well. She committed suicide by self-immolation, so whatever crazy thing you did after your last breakup, remember it's not as bad as setting yourself on fire (unless you set someone else on fire, which is also uncool). One-night stands were semi-justified in pre-Rome because men only left town back then to fight wars. Now dudes have one-night stands and leave the girl's apartment early to play Call of Duty with their roommates all day. The irony!

stories lined up with a specific view of Jesus Christ's teachings, except for the "Gospel According to Franklin," where "Jesus got some fly-ass bitches to attend a party us ugly guys threw! Let it be known, most people throw parties with a large number of lonely men, but this guy threw one where the ladies outnumbered the men three-to-one. He is clearly the Savior!" This gospel appears to have been tampered with.

What they wrote: the four gospels and some letters. Three of them sounded pretty similar and one (John) sounded nuts! The Council of Nicaea left that one in for kicks. These writers also wrote several post-Jesus texts, including one whole book devoted entirely to a description of what will happen to the Earth when Christ comes back. It's not as fun as it sounds, but there are dragons!

Famous quote: "Do unto others whatever you wish to have them do to you." Strangely this popular Golden Rule of treating others the way you wish to be treated backfired, since most people are masochistic psychos who are okay with doing terrible shit to people and having people do terrible shit to them in return.

Lucian

Lucian was a Greek comic orator from Rome who developed the first real stand-up routines and sketches about mythology and Plato, stealing from Woody Allen two thousand years before Woody was born.

What he wrote: several comedic speeches, including one that started with the classic stand-up opener, "Ladies and citizens, I just flew in from Crete, and boy did I see Icarus die." He later wrote a very controversial bit where he kept yelling, "I love Greek people, but I HATE Spartans!"

Famous quote: "Now I make the only true statement you are to expect—that I am a liar." Lucian was also lying about this, however, which made every head in Rome explode.

Ovid

Ovid was a Roman poet who wrote many erotic poems before writing about how mountains and trees change over time (this was also erotic to Romans, since they thought everything was erotic).

What he wrote: *The Metamorphoses*, some poems about tree ladies getting raped, which was the opposite of the movie *Evil Dead*, where a tree rapes a woman.

Famous quote: "A prince should be slow to punish and quick to reward." Ovid said this after being caught in bed with a prince's wife.

Also: "All love is vanquished by a succeeding love." From Ovid, trying to convince his jealous wife he didn't have feelings for his past lover, the prince's wife.

Marcus Aurelius

Marcus Aurelius was a Roman emperor who was also the most important Stoic philosopher. Stoics attempted to rid themselves of negative emotions. Unfortunately they counted empathy for peasant villagers on the list of negative emotions.

What he wrote: *Meditations*, an early Weight Watchers handbook about staying disciplined and taking care of a country without putting on pounds from the stress.

Famous quote: "And thou wilt give thyself relief, if thou doest every act of thy life as if it were the last." Marcus Aurelius didn't do much besides write notes to loved ones as if he were about to die, until everyone told him to tone it down.

St. Augustine

St. Augustine was a Catholic philosopher who wrote a book about his spicy, sinful youth, when he committed horrible atrocities like stealing a pear this one time.

What he wrote: *Confessions*, which can be summed up in four words: cities bad; country good. All the sin and depravity happen in cities, where people are anonymous and can sleep with whores whenever they feel like it. Unlike the country, where people are wholesome and only have sex with livestock.

Famous quote: "I consider that nothing so casts down the manly mind from its height as the fondling of a woman, and those bodily contacts." Catholics today still hide behind God's Will as a way of getting out of foreplay.

Old Norse Writers

Dragon-fighting, America-discovering, horned-helmet-wearing Vikings! Actually, those are all offensive stereotypes. The real Vikings were barbarian pirates who were constantly expanding and killing tons of people, while writing stories about how many people they were able to kill.

What they wrote: the Völsunga Saga, a story that was the early version of Disney's *Sword in the Stone*, except in this story the sword is placed inside a tree, so the stakes are way lower. Most of the characters today have been reappropriated as Final Fantasy Summon Spells.

Famous quote: "Where wolf's ears are, wolf's teeth are near." To which another viking responded, "Thank you, Captain Obvious!" before both Vikings were devoured by wolves.

St. Thomas Aquinas

A Catholic saint who spent an inordinately long time explaining ways to not have sex, St. Thomas Aquinas could have just said the missionary position was the only Christian way to have sex, but instead he went on long, heated rants about the number of creative un-Christian ways to have sex. Followers became uncomfortable, especially when he dedicated every sermon to listing weird fetish-y sex acts he had heard about that week in the confessional. He also thought masturbation was worse than rape, which says a lot about the people who still hold him in high regard.

What he wrote: Besides his diatribes on sex and the necessary killing of all heathens, St. Thomas Aquinas also wrote *The Five Proofs of God's Existence.* Here are a few of his first drafts that are easier to understand than the later versions:

- If things move, then someone moved them. I can't find my favorite quill pen. If everyone in this goddamned monastery said they didn't steal it, then God must have moved it. Therefore God is the great invisible mover of things. God exists. QED.
- Some things are greater than other things. For instance, we're better than slaves and womenfolk. They are lesser than humans. God also owns slaves. Those slaves are we. God exists. QED.
- I'm surrounded by stupid fucks. There are occasions when I find myself where stupid fucks are not present. God is the absence of stupid fucks. God exists and I pray I get to be with him soon! QED.

Famous quote: From a sermon on the wrong ways to have sex: "You have heard, dear brothers of the Faith, that it is difficult for a rich man to enter the Kingdom of Heaven, but I say to you, it is more difficult for any person who has attempted the 'Fassanova Scroll Licker' or the 'Rope-Tangled Stigmata,' which I'm told has something to do with using several appendages to please a woman during her unclean days. There will be no more of that!"

Dante Alighieri

Dante Alighieri was an Italian poet who wrote in terza rima, where one stanza steals a rhyme from the last, the same way Dante stole characters from older poems and used them in his own.

What he wrote: *Inferno*, which is about a guy's midlife crisis, except instead of buying a nice car and dating someone younger, the guy visits Hell to talk to a few people there.

Famous quote: "Abandon all hope, ye who enter here!" Dante stole this line from a note written on the door of his friend's outhouse. It was pretty funny.

Geoffrey Chaucer

Geoffrey Chaucer was an Old English poet whose writing is tantamount to a goofy Bruegel painting.[12]

What he wrote: Chaucer wrote *The Canterbury Tales*, which feature many drunk pilgrims sharing stories about whorish women with gaps in their teeth.

Famous quote: "Whan that Aprille with his shoores soote / the drought of March hath perced to the roote / And bathed every vein in swich liquor / Of which vertu engendred is the flour." You should already have this memorized if you want to fit in at Yale!

---

12. Wow. That didn't help. Picture a really funny *Where's Waldo?* with a lot of poor folk acting silly. Now you know both Bruegel and Chaucer.

Michel de Montaigne

Michel de Montaigne was a French writer and one of the first Skeptics, who represented a newfangled belief that you should only believe what can be proved empirically. Before that, everyone believed everything they heard, no matter what the source, which led to people blindly believing that frequent masturbation led to hairy palms and that witches caused all bad things.[13]

What he wrote: the first essay (French word for "try" as in "I tried really hard for this paper to mean something, but then I took a nap and finished it right before class").

Famous quote: "A wise man sees as much as he ought, not as much as he can." Montaigne learned this lesson after seeing a hermaphrodite jump over a fence revealing both sets of genitals.

Miguel de Cervantes

Spain's only great author, Miguel de Cervantes wrote a book claiming another author had written it while Cervantes merely translated the text, which seems really postmodern, but the real reason Cervantes did that was so no one would fear for his sanity after he had written a disturbingly long book.

What he wrote: *Don Quixote*, about an old man who stays up too late reading and goes crazy, and then pretends he is like the knights of yore. Now Don Quixote lives on in the form of trinkets on mantels.

Famous quote: "A private sin is not so prejudicial in this world, as a public indecency." From Cervantes' first court appearance. Many historians thought Cervantes was imprisoned for financial disputes,

---

13. Sadly, these two things are in fact true and were later proved empirically.

but, in fact, it was for showing his penis to everyone he saw in the street.

William Shakespeare

William Shakespeare is the most famous writer in the English language. People pay homage to his poetry and plays by reading one or two in high school. The plays are full of sex, murder, and suicide, the three subjects most commonly cited for banning a book in high school, but Shakespeare gets a pass. That's how adored Shakespeare is! He makes uptight people okay with teaching their kids about murder and suicide.

What he wrote: *Hamlet*, a play featuring suicide, matricide, fratricide, accidental geronticide, parricide, and planticide. The only thing that doesn't die in this play is the ghost of Hamlet's dad, making this the most frightening play ever written.

Famous quote: "All the world's a stage, / and the men and women merely players. / Some are orcs, some are fairies, / but in our own way we are all dragon-slayers." Shakespeare got really into LARPing in his later writings.

Isaac Newton

As my high school teacher used to say: "Millions of people saw an apple and said 'applesauce,' while Newton saw gravity. Which was more important?" Probably applesauce. What did gravity ever do to accent the delicious taste of pork chops? People rejected Newton's theories and while eating the worst kind of food they had—the fig—they would say, "This fig puts as bad a taste in my mouth as Newtonian physics!" and that's how we got the name Fig Newton.

What he wrote: *Mathematical Principals of Natural Philosophy*, which famously states that "For every action there is an equal and opposite reaction." Newton discovered this basis for physics while in a heated argument with a roommate over some food that had been taken from Isaac's icebox. The roommate said Isaac was "overreacting," to which Isaac said, "I am reacting just as much as I've been wronged! A ham sandwich's worth of spite!"

Famous quote: "I can calculate the motion of heavenly bodies, and right now, baby, your body's looking like it wants to gravitate over to the largest object in this room! Me." (Classic Newtonian pickup line.)

Honore de Balzac

Honore de Balzac was a French writer, born in Tours, France. He had a terrible first day in school when his teacher mispronounced his name as "Balsac?" All the children laughed because "Balsac" in French means "ball sack."

What he wrote: books about post-Napoleon France, which wasn't nearly as fun without all the beheadings and bathtub stabbings.

Famous quote: "Chance, my dear, is the sovereign Deity in childbearing." Balzac used this reasoning with a lady after refusing to pull out.

Charles Darwin

Darwin was a scientist who traveled the world to find out what made species of animals so varied.

What he wrote: *The Origin of Species*, proving that all creatures on Earth descended from other creatures. Christians denied that people descended from a primate ancestor, and said they'd rather believe that people were made out of clay by a three-tier deity who always existed and created the Earth from nothingness, and who was also the son of a virgin and a ghost-dove who exists inside every human, which makes way more sense.

Famous quote: "Animals, whom we have made our slaves, we do not like to consider our equal." Referring to all animals other than his pug, whom Darwin treated better than most of his kids.

Sigmund Freud

Freud was the man who seeded a progeny of doctors interested in abnormal psychology. With the intellectual force of a battering ram, Freud penetrated deeply into the untouched and delicate flower that was psychosis. His strong, trunk-like stature as an analyst led to the cherry popping of many previously unthought theories on the mind. He also proved that people constantly think about sex even while not penis reading about it.

What he wrote: *On Dreams*, a short paper about Freud forgetting to write his paper *On Dreams* in time for publication and how his disappointed father and gym teacher laughed at him while he was in his underwear in front of all his peers. Also *Civilization and Its Discontents*, which proposes that society sets up rules that constantly burden our natural instincts to rape and kill. This made many people uncomfortable, especially when everyone was asked to agree/disagree with Freud's assumption "on the count of three," and literally everyone on the planet agreed at the same time that they had had rape and murder fantasies. Life continued as usual, but things were very tense for about a week or two.

Famous quote: "America is a mistake, a giant mistake." When Freud said "America," he was mostly referring to everything white people did in the United States, except, of course, the making of *Die Hard* and *Die Hard with a Vengeance*.

Bertrand Russell

Bertrand Russell was a mathematician and notable atheist. Right after destroying mathematic axioms in a few thousand pages, he took on the task of debunking religion by writing a single sentence: "Saying God exists because you can't prove otherwise is like saying there's a china teapot in orbit near Mars but you can't see it with telescopes." This, as most people know, ended the debate on religion forever.

What he wrote: gobs of books, mostly about how old math axioms weren't necessarily correct and that war is wrong. Ha! I just summed up a thousand of your books in a sentence, Bertrand!

Famous quote: "Do not fear to be eccentric in opinion, for every opinion that is now accepted was once eccentric." Russell said this while telling his wife why it was okay that he liked watching "dancing bear" porn.

Albert Einstein

The smartest human being who ever lived, Albert Einstein used his genius to split the atom and flirt with redheads.

What he wrote: Einstein wrote the Special Theory of Relativity, which argued that time is relative to motion, which led Einstein to the brilliant conclusion "It's five o'clock somewhere" before taking a drink at eleven in the morning.

Famous quote: Einstein famously did not speak during his youth, until one day he said: "This soup is cold." His mother was baffled and asked why he hadn't spoken before, to which he replied: "Because up until now everything was fine, you filthy woman! Now, go heat up this soup, ya old bag!" Historians often edit out the part where he was mean to his mom.

Jean-Paul Sartre

An existential philosopher and writer, Jean-Paul Sartre spoke and wrote about how he lived for the sake of other humans, then wrote a play about how much he hated other humans.

What he wrote: Sartre wrote *Being and Nothingness*, which alleged that all there is in the world is what we see, nothing more. Sartre's episode of *Celebrity Ghost Story* is awful, since he just keeps saying, "There's no way to really say it was supernatural or not, so I'm not going to speculate whether what I saw was a ghost or not. But it probably wasn't a ghost . . ."

Famous quote: "Hell is other people." Sartre discovered this fact while playing Monopoly with his wife.

Danielle Steel

Danielle Steel managed to put the same shit in a different order (and possibly different locale) twice a year for her entire writing career.

What she wrote: *Echoes*, a book about finding love in the strangest of places, and *The Wedding*, a book about finding love in the strangest of places.

Famous quote: "A bad review is like baking a cake with all the best ingredients and having someone sit in it." Whenever Danielle Steel makes a cake, it's undercooked and filled with sugary ingredients taken from previous cakes.

The Guy Who Wrote the Movie *Torque*

Little is known about Matt Johnson, the man, however his films (directed one, wrote two) are studied in all film schools as the benchmark for great cinema.

What he wrote: the movie *Torque*. In the same way some avant-garde poets mimic the structure of mathematical equations in their pieces, Matt Johnson, writer/visionary, used the formula for torque (that is "$t = r \times F$" where r is the length of the lever arm and F is the force around a rotational point) as a starting point for his now famous screenplay *Torque*. Johnson saw how this formula could be used in a three-act structure: where the level of enjoyment for an audience is equal to the number of really fast motorcycles times the number of beer bottles arbitrarily thrown behind someone's head. How right he was! Sadly, critics were hesitant to give *Torque* perfect reviews, as no one had ever seen anything like it in over one hundred years of cinema and everyone worried the general public might not be ready to accept such a cerebral masterpiece.

Famous quote: "I just jumped my bike onto the roof of a moving train. It's amazing what you can do when you have no choice." This subtle dialogue concerning predestination and the life of a biker are prevalent throughout the film.

The Guy Who First Said "At the End of the Day . . ."

A hero to those who never could see past their entire day and truly gain perspective on what they were doing, either in their personal lives or at work. Like the koans of ancient Buddhist texts, this small phrase continues to baffle and awe the most contemplative among us.

What he wrote: "At the end of the day . . ."

Famous quote: "At the end of the day, you know, it is what it is and what's good for the goose is good for the gander."[14]

---

14. Now would be a nice time to go out and buy another copy of this book so I never have to go back to an office job where someone says bullshit like this.

The Future of Books

Soon, HBO will condense the few books worth reading into a six-part miniseries that can be downloaded and watched while you're on your commute to work. After that, physical books will only be sold as collector's items via infomercials on QVC. They'll be sold the same way they sell commemorative plates, except instead of depicting cute pictures of children playing on seesaws, books will feature images of people like Meursault (aka *The Stranger*) in front of a condemning jury. That will really lighten up a room! Thanks, books!

The only booklike texts people will read in the future will be crowdsourced stories written sentence by sentence on the Internet.[15] Everyone will be much happier with these stories since every person will have had a hand in writing them! The death of reading physical books written by one person is good for any healthy democracy since reading one sole person's ideas is fascist and un-American.[16] Also, when books are over and done, we can focus our energy on other, worthwhile future activities, like the right way to build a fire and which parts of the "infected" are suitable for eating.[17]

---

15. Opening lines from a famous future book written by three separate people: "If you don't like Lucky Charms, you can GTFO! nuff sad. LOL, bt forserious IDK ne1 who hate LCs."

16. I should mention that America still runs everything in the future, though America will be run by China.

17. Right! I should also mention that most of us become zombies.

CHAPTER THREE

Getting Started

Where Can I Find Books Now?

ince some people will require proof that you possess the books you're pretending to read, it is important to know where books exist in the world. This section will help you discover where to find books and what pitfalls to look out for while obtaining one.

It's hard to warn someone about the dangers of books, especially by doing so in a book, so I'm going to do this as simply and painlessly as possible: in a Choose Your Own Adventure format. Since you've already read for hours, the following section will be a much deserved break from the monotony of this guide so far. Feel free to flip through this Choose Your Own Adventure as many times as you'd like and figure out which course of action works best for you.

Quest for the Last Bound Books:
A Choose Your Own Adventure

You are sitting at your kitchen table preparing for a small party. You are struck by the thought that aside from your learned social graces and exceptionally well-toned body, you have nothing to impress your guests with.

"What were those decorations that make your brain look smart?" you say aloud. "Oh, yes! Books! How could I forget!" Planning to distract people from the fact that you are an ornate but empty jewelry box's human equivalent, you realize you have no idea where to begin!

You walk outside into the cold October drizzle, thinking of a place where you last saw a book. You realize the weather is nice enough to walk somewhere. At the same moment you realize that you will most likely never know true love, but, as usual, you bury the thought deep underneath your mental list of errands. You remember there is a used bookstore a few blocks away. The regular bookstore and the library are also options, as is returning to your house to order books online.

If you'd like to walk to the nearby used bookstore, turn to the next page.

If you'd like to drive to the regular new-books bookstore, turn to page 46.

If you'd like to drive to a library, turn to page 48.

If you'd like to order a book using the Internet, turn to page 49.

While walking to the local indie bookstore, you recall that several fatal wolf attacks have occurred in your neighborhood. No one who has been attacked has survived, except one person who ran away while throwing large pieces of meat behind him. You remember that you have several large pieces of raw beef in your pocket for snacking. As you pace quickly toward the calming maroon awning of the bookstore, you hear the sound of several paws patting the ground behind you. When you turn around, a pack of wolves are approaching quickly. You reach in your pocket for the chunks of raw meat.

If you decide to rip your shirt off and rub the meat on your chest, then stupidly fight *a pack of wolves* with your bare hands while reeking of dead mammal, turn to the next page.

If you decide to fling the meat toward the street in order to distract the wolves while quickly running into the bookstore for safety, turn to page 44.

Are you FUCKING kidding me? You chose to fight wolves with your bare hands? How much clearer does the story have to be for you to realize that this is a terrible choice? Seriously. A fucking child could figure this out. You get one more shot at this:

To not choose the dumbest course of action, go back a page and try again, or

To fight the wolves, go to the next page.

You are eaten by wolves.

The last thing you see before you pass out from blood loss is the owner of the bookstore with a confused look on his face (he's trying to figure out whether to call the police and save you, or do the world a favor by letting you die, since, should you survive what he just saw you do, you will certainly be responsible for the death of many in the future).

Don't bother going back to the beginning of the book to start over. You'll probably just pick the same ending anyway.

You have died.

You fling the raw meat into the street, where the wolves devour it. You quickly open the door to the Undercover Bookstore. The smell of dust and cat dander hits your nose like a predator drone shooting every which way in your nasal cavity.

"How's it going?" you say to the clerk, and close the door. The man behind the counter looks up from his crossword puzzle without moving his head. You see that he looks like a mix between Darwin and Karl Marx with the jowls and facial expressions of a Saint Bernard. He clears his throat, then goes back to work on his crossword puzzle. You walk a few steps before starting to sneeze.

"Cat allergies," you say to the man at the register, but he looks annoyed and confused, as if to say, "Cat? What cat?"

You walk toward the back of the store, where there's a Fiction and Literature section. *Yes*, you think, *that's what I want to read! Fiction.* The books on the shelves look somewhere between thirty to two hundred years old. "Used books," you say to yourself, remembering a time when books had monetary value and people could trade them for money. That's strange. You've never seen anyone enter this store. Where did all these books come from? The titles are in no discernible order and seem to have not moved from their places on the shelves since your town's founding. You slide a book from the shelf, some Russian author you have never heard of.

You carry the book to the register. Marx Saint Bernard appears to be asleep, but when you clear your throat, he opens one eyelid and waves you away. Confused, you take the book and walk outside, making sure before you open the door that no wolves are waiting to pounce.

You walk back to your house.

You get into bed and begin reading your new book. It's full of mysterious characters and talking cats. You start to feel tired.

If you'd like to close the book and take a nap, go to the next page.

If you'd like to sit up and read through the entire book right away, go to page 51.

As you drift to sleep, you see some kind of smoke (or is that your imagination?) coming from the pages of the old book.

When you wake up, you're being held in the strong arms of a man. You look up to see the bearded face of the bookstore owner. You try to yell but all that comes out is a screeching cat noise! You look down and see your paws and orange fur. You have become a cat! How did this happen? How many people in your town have been turned into cats by this store owner? Is everyone in this town part pet?

Though you ponder whether or not every used bookstore is secretly run by an old wizard intent on casting shape-shifting spells on his patrons, you eventually understand that being a bookstore cat has its benefits: You get to sprawl out on the bestsellers you think customers should not buy, you can sleep wherever you want (including on top of the cash register so no one can buy anything!), and when you're bored, you can scratch the faces of bratty kids who annoy you. What a life!

The only problem is that whenever you leave the store, you are chased by the local pack of wolves. Eventually, while you're rooting through the Dumpster for tuna cans, the wolves get the jump on you, and you are eaten.

Your last word is "MEOOWWWWWW!"

You have died.

You get in your car and drive down toward the Treetop Commons, where the Bed Bath &Beyond is. You're almost certain there was some kind of new-books bookstore near there. As you pull into the parking lot, you notice a store with tall letters on the front: a bookstore. You were right! You've made it.

As you enter the bookstore, a rush of AC comes barreling on top of your head like the cold ghost of your disapproving grandfather. What would he say about wasting time on nonsense like books? Your body senses the existential fright even if your mind fails to articulate it. You shake the negativity away and walk to a table of "New Releases."

The sheer number of books makes you feel small. At the same time, the store's colors are calming and lull you into a euphoric, anxiety-free mood. An old soul singer's album moves through the building like the mist from a pleasant cooking smell in an old cartoon. The last time you remember feeling this good involved painkillers after a dental surgery.

This place is beautiful, but how long have I been here? you think. You look around for a clock but see none. You reach for a cat calendar from the bargain rack and relax for a moment until you realize that the year on the calendar is 2075. Your head starts spinning. A man in a trench coat passes by, muttering to himself about a book killing his father. You need to get out, and fast!

You consider returning home book-free but just before you walk out the door, you see a book you were told to read years ago.

If you'd like to go home for that night's party book-free and bake a large ham for your guests, go to the next page.

If you'd like to buy a book, take it home and start reading, go to page 51.

You arrive home, and in order to distract your friends from the house's lack of literature, you bake a large ham. The ham comes out moist and sweet, and while you're eating a piece of it, you have one clear, final thought: *Life doesn't get any better than this.* You slip into a food coma while watching a soap opera. You do not move from the couch for what seems like days, and time blankets itself around you like so much fondue.

For some reason, you can't remember your guests arriving or leaving your party. When you finally shake yourself from the malaise of the ham you baked, it's far too late to recover. You are now eighty-seven years old. Your children are grown up and living with their own families making similarly terrible decisions. The last thing you hear before your heart calmly disregards the rest of your body forever is a faint voice whispering something unintelligible in your ear. "What's that?" you mumble. "Rooks? Crooks?" You'll never know.

You have died.

You drive to the library. You step inside and see that it is bustling with people.

Oh, right. The library, you think, where anyone can relax and expand his or her mind. You notice that "anyone" includes only children, the homeless, and the nearly deceased. You also see that "expanding your mind" doesn't mean reading, but rather looking at porn on a computer or talking to yourself. You can feel the dust on the marble floor through your shoes, as if you were the first person stepping on the surface of the moon.

You walk through several rows of books and see tens if not hundreds of books you were supposed to read in school, as well as books you've always heard smart people talk about.

When you ask a librarian how "this whole operation works," she is a bit confused, then says you can take as many as fifteen books out at a time . . . for free!

What suckers, you think, as you pile random books into your arms. *Now everyone at my party will think I'm smart and I didn't have to spend a cent!* You laugh maniacally for ten solid minutes, and no one reacts, even though it sounds as though you've plotted the assassination of a superhero. An eerie sense of looming despair sweeps over you as a librarian scans each book.

You go home and begin reading.

Go to page 51.

You go inside and turn on your computer. You search briefly for a highly rated bestseller on a website and click the "purchase" button. Satisfied, you go into your living room to see what's on TV.

At your party that night, several guests ask why you haven't yet read the current bestselling novel that everyone in the world but you has apparently read. You assure them the book is in the mail "as we speak," then present a plate of your famous mini-quiches to shut them up. You put the book out of your mind and enjoy the party.

Three days later the doorbell rings when you're not expecting visitors. *Who could that be?* It's the mailman with a package for you in a cardboard box. You look skeptically at the box's cryptic features the way a dog would a stranger who entered its home. *Is someone trying to kill me or send me a gift? There could be anything from anthrax to a care package from my mother in here!* You do a mental recount of your mortal enemies and then weigh that list against the number of loved ones you have. You decide it's about fifty-fifty and open the box. Inside you find a book in plastic wrap.

"Oh, right," you say to yourself, "this thing."

You sit down on the couch and begin reading the blurbs on the back of the book. You see that Stephen King liked this particular novel. Didn't Stephen King write that book about the evil clown? You turn on your computer and look up Stephen King's bibliography. That's so many books! Too many to read in this lifetime.

If you prefer not to read anything at all and start playing your favorite computer game instead, go to the next page.

If you'd like to start reading the book, go to page 51.

You start playing your favorite online computer game. The game becomes all you do in your spare time, and you buy each new edition of the game on newer, faster computers until your home becomes a technological cocoon that only you can fit in. A few more years pass, and you find out the newest edition of your favorite game will come with a small plug that fits snugly around the stem of your brain. You buy it immediately, relishing how far human technology has come. When you hook the game up directly to your brain, it's like nothing you've ever experienced. Bright colors and good feelings wash over you. You are constantly the center of attention no matter where the game takes you. You're so enthralled that you never think to remove yourself from the game to take a break.

In the dead of night, small robots enter your home. You are still playing the game, wide awake, but have no sense of your physical surroundings. The robots begin harvesting your vital organs to make machine-human hybrids in preparation for their first onslaught on the human race.

The machines have won.

You have died.

You start reading like you've never read before. You decide not to do anything that night but read until you're ready for bed, and when you finally fall asleep that night, you dream, for the first time, of something other than a vague and imageless doom. You're having thoughts, and your mind can finally make pictures without the help of a TV!

You read and read and read. Inspired by one book, you go on to the next. Your coworkers and family notice how often you're willing to share your thoughts, which seem to be nearly comprehensible to other humans. You read anything you can find: text messages, stop signs, embroidered quilts. You start to slink away from society to finish a few books. First a long one you heard was decent. Then a few more in a week's time. Your friends and family now feel the need to intervene. "I shall not be taken down by you fraudulent phonies!" you shout at them.

You attempt to convert others to the cult of reading, but fail. Like a great literary Cassandra (you keep insisting), you can see the future of thought but are powerless to stop it no matter how loudly you present these predictions to the public. You wind up as miserable and alone as you would have had you stayed home that fateful day when you chose to find a book. Only now you can articulate the utter pointlessness of your life using words. You revel in the irony that in your attempt to know more about the world through reading, you only found out frightening facts about your inner self, like being able to recognize love as a man-made verbal construct inspired by a need to explain a sudden abundance of dopamine in the brain. The last thing you think before a sudden aneurism strips you of your motor functions is, *Death, be not proud!*

At least you can now quote poetry.

You have died.

CHAPTER FOUR

A Guide to Finding Books by Section

I f you survived the last section, you know that people die alone no matter what, and that it's best to spend quality time with your family and friends as much as possible before you transcend this earthly existence. If you still think finding a book is important, however, you're going to need more direct advice on how to select the correct book in a store or library. Committing to a specific book is like committing to anything else in life: If it feels wrong after a few minutes, quit forever. So, in order to save you a few more minutes before choosing a book to not finish, I'll guide you through each section so you can avoid wasting all your brain fuel on discerning what phrases like "graphic novel" mean.[1]

Bookstores and libraries have several signs to let you know the genre of book located in particular sections. But for those of us who do not

---

1. An oxymoron since "graphic" refers to intense violence or descriptive sex scenes in a movie, whereas "novel" refers to longwinded banal storytelling.

have the superhuman memory to store tens of definitions in our heads, here are a few translations and what you'll find in each:

Classics, or the "Every Book You Never Finished But Speak at Length About When Brought Up" Section

The word "classics" usually refers to Greek and Roman literature but has come to mean literature that, when you have read it, makes you a sanctimonious shitbag. Luckily, I can present to you the gist of these "great books" without the side effect of your becoming a loathsome human version of a *Fowler's English Usage*.[2]

Classics are any book that perfectly encapsulates the work's genre and can be considered a great work by any era's standard. Or, as we define it now, any book you were supposed to read in high school. If you read magazines and newspapers, you are, in fact, smarter than everyone you know. But if you've read anything from the Classics section you will feel superior to everyone, and that's more important.

Classics Subgenres

Greek and Latin

Love war, but are afraid to admit it? Read poetry about it! Not that lame-ass Wilfred Owen shit, but the original use of "*Dulce Et Decorum*

It is sweet and right...

---

2. Imagine Strunk and White's *Elements of Style* but add a disdainful "you write like a *child*!" to every sentence. Or imagine that your grandfather were alive and looking over your shoulder as you type anything. That's *Fowler's*.

Est,"[3] when dying for your country was as fun and as common as drinking absinthe while the sun was still up.

English Novelists and Essayists

Most English essays were concerned with Britain's burden to bring civilization to all those dumb countries that weren't acting British enough. These ideas led to several wars and, in turn, many books about those wars.

In the English novel, characters explore boring non-war subjects like (a) "Why am I so rich?" (b) "Why am I so poor?" and (c) "Why do I feel Jewish?" Even when there were good wars to write about, writers such as Jane Austen wrote novels concerning marriage. They usually went like this:

"You're being a real jerk."

"Sorry about that. I was secretly helping you."

"Oh, you're wonderful! And you have so much money! You're my new favorite cousin!"

"Let's get married."

The End.

Russian Novels

If you're anything like me, you walk the streets late at night, eating nothing but slices of deli meat, muttering to yourself, and drinking hard liquor in large quantities. You are constantly setting up bets inside your own brain that only involve you and imagined humans, and when you win those bets, you tally them up as reasons you beat the universe at its own game! When you finally open up and tell a stranger these thoughts, you frighten that person and he runs away.

Congratulations: You are one card game away from being the main

---

3. Translation: "War is awesome."

character in a Russian novel. These books also feature a guy challenging people to duels by slapping them with an empty glove, über-literate people who are misunderstood by society so they share their feelings with prostitutes, and constant visions of the devil. We can all relate, right?

The Great American Novel
Sprawling, Bible-influenced stories about greedy racists and why America is "so great!" even after thousands of pages exploring why it is not that great.

Books Some Dude in the Bookstore Keeps Calling "Classic"
This guy's an idiot. His taste sways with the wind, and half the time he's only ironically liking the book. If it seems un-ironic, he's talking about Kurt Vonnegut.

Required Reading

Mostly fiction aimed at getting high schoolers to ruin the only real summer vacations they'll ever experience.

Who You'll See in the Classics Section

Recent graduates of college who are now unemployed or retired people.

Books You'll Find in the Classics Section

Crime and Punishment: If you hate your landlord and are looking for the right course of vengeful action, this is the book for you!

Jane Austen's *Pride and Prejudice*: If you think quiet men are sexy (instead of, rightfully, thinking they're boring), this is the book for you!

Les Misérables: If you listen to Broadway musicals while reading anyway, this is the book for you!

The Grapes of Wrath: If you like the deaths featured in the game Oregon Trail 2, this is the book for you!

Ulysses: If you think postmodern meta-literary descriptions of pooping and sex are fun, this is the book for you!

A NOTE ABOUT CLASSIC NOVELS

Classics often feature narratives framed in the form of letters. To give you an idea what these books were about, here are some letters written back to main characters who wrote letters in these texts:

Frankenstein

My Dearest Robert,

I just received your 4 pound, 235-page letter. I was happy to know how you're feeling on the North Pole (say hello to old St. Nick if you see him!) but if you're really looking for a friend, perhaps you should ask more questions? Just a thought. Don't you ever wonder what deeds your dear old sister is up to? I know it's exciting up there with all that ice to stare at, but I'm a person, too! I've been sewing my own dresses lately. And I'm teaching myself how to knit.

I apologize for not writing earlier but it took me six days to finish reading your letter, which I read most of while walking through the garden in this dreadful heat! I tried reading some to your niece and nephew. This got a little weird when you started writing about a zombie who kills children. Really, Robert! Is that necessary? It appears as though your cabin fever has led you to devise a nightmarish tale of a man creating a monster in his own image. We don't need to compose an entire serial inspired by your insecurities about becoming a father, do we? If you don't want to have a child, just tell Father and he'll still support your little science expe-

ditions regardless! He knows as well as I do creating progeny is overrated. These little time-consuming bastards!

Anywho, hope you're not too long up there! Stay warm.

Your loving sister,

Margaret

The Sorrows of a Young Werther

Dear Werther,

Seriously? Just move. There are plenty of other fish in the sea, as they say. Fish that don't make you want to kill yourself. You're making a terrible mistake by only pursuing one woman. She's clearly into you, but she's taken. TAKEN. Move on. Come down to the beer garden with me and we'll find someone for you. She could look just like Lotte. Lord knows most Germans are inbred and end up looking like everyone else anyway.

I've read every letter you've written to me, but sometimes I feel like you're repeating yourself. I know the seasons change. Please write to me about something else! Also keep this in mind: Lotte is not worth dying for. You will meet other people. Someday, I predict there will be a place where we can write all our interests down (what music we like, what places we frequent) and everyone will be able to see each other's shared interests, and women, all kinds of women from different countries even, will begin a correspondence with us based on these likes and dislikes. They'll be able to see where we work, live, and attended school. And we'll be able to see salacious photographs of them at the beach! All for the purpose of courting! Then we'll have so many choices it will be impossible to settle down.

So remember that next time you think about offing yourself over one lady. She's not even that interesting, Werther! She plays piano, sure, but guess who else does . . . Every fucking person I know. There's nothing else to do besides play piano and read letters. So let's take it down a notch, shall we? And meet me at the garden this weekend to check out these fine bitches living down the street.

Your friend,

Wilhelm

Dracula

Dear Jonathan, or should I say: Dear guy who's dumb enough to go to the castle where the monsters clearly live!

I just read your diary. For fuck's sake, this is a joke, right? There was a whole town telling you there's something weird happening at the castle and you still go there? Someone handed you a crucifix—a FUCKING crucifix—for protection and you still went? Are you kidding me?? You should have never tried to help this asshole buy a house in London. Then he would live there. Near people we know. You should have told him to move to Paris. Those freaks love deadly sex-monsters. Anyway, I'm pissed. You could have told me all this before you got stuck up there in that castle and I became a slave to an undead people-eater. You're a dope. You also forgot to take the garbage out AGAIN! I was a fool to marry someone who could not see the writing on the wall. Writing that said, "A Vampire Definitely Lives in This Castle." You make me fucking sick.

Your stupid wife,

Mina

The Perks of Being a Wallflower

Dear Anonymous Person who keeps leaving notes for me,

I don't know who told you I was a good person, but I'm not. You sound like a real pussy. Now cheer up and watch some funny TV for a change. You're wearing me out with all this sad shit.

Sincerely,

Some Person

Nonfiction, or the "I Feel Smarter Just for Buying This" Section

Nonfiction is for people who don't have time for those dumb make-'em-ups that people keep talking about. Instead, nonfiction books answer important questions about the real world, like "How tall was Teddy Roosevelt?" and "How did this reality star get a goddamned book deal?" Unlike fiction, some of these books take upward of six hundred hours to read. You'll hear readers in this section saying things like "Oh, did you pick up the new Philip Roth? Well, I'll be reading about one battalion in the Civil War for the rest of my life."

Nonfiction Subgenres

True Crime

Do you love watching *Law & Order* but don't want the self-hatred that comes with watching nine hours of TV in a row? Read a book about *real* murders for thirty to forty hours. That's nearly a full-time job's worth of contemplating the murder of innocent people, without any commercials interrupting the darkness that will eventually consume you.

Biographies

Long explanations of how famous people became famous, listing all the opportunities they had that you did not, solidifying your assertion that you will never be famous.[4]

Memoirs

Just like biographies except they're untrue.

History

Everything you never wanted to know about Genghis Khan! Before you buy a book from this section, look at the size of the book. Just feel it in

---

4. I have never finished one of these, though I have purchased hundreds, so while I can't tell you anything interesting from a famous person's life, I can tell you where many famous people's parents met.

your hands. Now think about what you're doing this year *besides* reading, because that's going to get in the way of a three-thousand-page book on one battle in the Pacific during World War II. Are you sure you didn't mean to just watch *Midway* the movie? Come to think of it, watching that whole movie is a big commitment, too.

Current Events

Buying a nonfiction book like *Too Big to Fail* or *The 9/11 Commission Report* is a lot like saying, "I'm gonna get to the bottom of my country's problems and only a few years after the damage has been done!" You get to read hundreds of pages of seemingly relevant information about a crisis, the real reasons for which will not be sorted out until fifty years after the book was published, and then you'll have to buy that book and not finish that one either.

Who You'll See in the Nonfiction Section

Forlorn single moms with nothing else to do with their afternoons. Also old men and future serial killers researching their predecessors.

Books You'll Find in the Nonfiction Section

The Rise and Fall of the Third Reich: Just like the History Channel, only it requires six times as many naps to get through.

A Brief History of Time: Stephen Hawking's simplification of why the known universe exists: elephants and turtles decided to put the world on their backs.

A Heartbreaking Work of Staggering Genius: Dave Eggers's list of every cool thing he's ever done.

Reference, or the "Great Resources for Writers and Other Dickheads Who Pretend to Know Everything" Section

Reference books will help you write poetry faster, or provide you with famous quotes so you can organize your humor book by reading the short thoughts of smart people.

Who You'll See in the Reference Section

High school students looking up pictures of dicks in *The Book of Nursing*. Someone thinking about purchasing a quote book before realizing the Internet exists and you don't need a $45 book to look quotes up.

Books You'll Find in the Reference Section

Dictionary: Samuel Johnson was the writer of the first dictionary, which he wrote by walking around asking people what words meant. Disappointed with their definitions, he put the commoners of Britain in his more scathing sentences. Definition of "dumb": "n. a person or thing having all the qualities of being from Staffordshire. Example: Everyone I know from Staffordshire is a fucking dumb inbred idiot!" Samuel Johnson's dictionary also featured a few words he only used while by himself, which led to a lot of confusion when he claimed that a universal word for a certain part of the male anatomy was "dangle-doo."

MLA Formatting and Style Guide: Every college student will own this book and diligently use it as an elbow rest while writing papers.

Thesaurus: Every time a high school student wants to impress someone without really knowing anything, a thesaurus gets its wings.

Self-Help, or the "I'm Spiritual, Not Religious" Section

Full of books written by experts in the field of writing self-help books, the Self-Help section can help you achieve anything from making a list of goals in your head to writing that list of goals on a piece of paper. Some self-help books appear to be about becoming a better boss or a better partner in a marriage, but every self-help book has at least one shared aim: to steal money from you.[5] Most of these books have a picture of the author smiling on the front. That's because every author of a self-help book wants you to look right in the face of the person screwing you out of $25.

Who You'll See in the Self-Help Section

Out-of-work actors trying to "get their shit together."

Books You'll Find in the Self-Help Section

The Secret by Rhonda Byrne: a phenomenon in publishing for its ability to force those who have not read it to immediately stop talking to those who have.

Malcom Gladwell's *Blink*: a book about how your brain might serve you better if you thought less. Reading this book makes you think more about thinking less, causing a temporary lapse in sanity which leaves you wondering why you ever tried to read this book in the first place.

---

5. This book, however, is totally different because this book is helping you avoid those other ones. Right? Dear LORD. I've become the thing I hate most!

Graphic Novels and Comics, or the "Emotionally, If Not Literally, I Still Live with My Parents" Section

Books that are mostly made up of pictures instead of words! Perfect!

Graphic Novels and Comics Subgenres

Manga

These books are just like anime except without the risk of hearing horrible English voice dubbing or having an epileptic seizure.

Comic Books

Superheroes appear in serialized, full-color picture books. Unlike children's picture books, however, comics are . . . comics have . . . well they're violent and sometimes there's swearing and girls with huge boobs. So comics are children's books with big boobs and violence. Also comic book fans will berate you for not knowing everything about a comic book character, whereas a child will only berate you with awkward questions about the boobs and violence they saw in comic books.

Graphic Novels

Just like comic books except the invisible supervillain haunting each book is imminent depression. Whether it's about a rough breakup and forsaking religion (*Blankets*), the Holocaust (*Maus*), or just how shitty and depressing everyday life is without horrific emotional events (*American Splendor*), graphic novels' sole aim is to make you sad. You know what the Green Lantern can't control? The Blues.[6] That's why he stays in comics and avoids the sadness of graphic novels.

Who You'll See in the Graphic Novels and Comics Section

The following is a verbatim transcription of something I heard in this section:

> *NO, they're not COMIC BOOKS, Mom. That's like calling my complete set of imported Cowboy Bebop Statues "toys," which, by the way, you do when my friends are around and it's really embarrassing! No, they're not action figures. Action figures have points of articulation, and statues do not. GOD! How many times do I have to tell you that? So, this is a book. This counts as a book, MOM! Why does every book have to be about what women felt like in England a million years ago? This book is by Neil Gaiman, and it's about a demigod named Dream who controls sleep and who gets trapped in the real world so the dreamworld falls apart and it's über-referential to other myths and legends, including the original Sandman, Wesley— MOM! Are you even listening? Buy this one so I can read it and finish it and we can split some free Pizza Hut after I fill out my BOOK IT! card. Thanks. Thanks, Mom. This is a really good book. Yes. Happy Mother's Day. What's that? Don't be silly, I'll drive.*

(This is both awesome and terrifying. Pause now for a moment to stand and applaud this book.)

---

6. In case any comic nerds are reading this, I KNOW: The Green Lantern only has trouble moving yellow objects. Please don't send me emails about the nerd cred I just lost.

Books You'll Find in the Graphic Novels and Comics Section

The Akira series: A guy uses telekinesis to his advantage, so it's just like Matilda except—DEAR GOD—he becomes an amorphous atomic bomb fetus that destroys Neo-Tokyo in a way that reminds everyone of World War II.

Chris Ware's *Jimmy Corrigan: The Smartest Kid on Earth*: Ever think your dad is mean or distant? Read this, then go give him a hug.

Charles Burns's *Black Hole*: Like the movie *Dazed and Confused* but instead of having one last good kegger, everyone contracts a flesh-altering STD.

American Splendor: A long reminder to never move to Cleveland.

Theater and Film, or the "I Wish I'd Studied Something Lucrative in College" Section

From Broadway spectacles to plays where the actor is instructed to actually poop onstage, the theater section offers some of the most daring[7] writing in print.

Who You'll See in the Theater and Film Section

Out-of-work actors trying to "get their shit together."

---

7. (i.e., "bad")

Books You'll Find in the Theater and Film Section

Constantin Stanislavski's *An Actor Prepares*: an instructional guide for actors to use their emotional memories to perform a role onstage. This system of acting has caused a few outbursts during performances. Such was the case when Sean "Puffy" Combs was in *A Raisin in the Sun* and accidentally said "R.I.P. Biggie Smalls" during an emotional scene.

Neil Labute's *In the Company of Men*: Remember when you thought sexism was waning? Well, it's back!

David Mamet's *Glengarry, Glen Ross*: Some old salesmen say "fuck" over and over.

Essays, or the "Extremely Genuine and Vulnerable Writing by People Who Are Probably Snarky Pricks in Real Life" Section

This section features ruminations on serious social issues and headaches. And that's just Joan Didion! Unlike interesting stories about poverty and struggle, essays usually begin with a first sentence about a distinctly upper-class problem, such as the following: "We borrowed my sister's car for the drive up to Martha's Vineyard that year; so foreign the car's make, though it was molded in Detroit, where our father grew up." That's a lot of information for someone to get through before deciding to stop reading! Why not just make the first sentence something like "I spend most of my spare time reading other essays"? Then readers of your essay will know to stop right away since they have nothing in common with the writer.

Who You'll See in the Essays Section

Women looking for a copy of *Bird by Bird*, so they can finally read it and get back to never writing anything.

Books You'll Find in the Essays Section

The White Album by Joan Didion: California is a great place for a mental breakdown.

Susan Sontag's *On Photography*: Visual media allow us to see the entire world from our homes, but images also numb us to human suffering. Sontag ends the essay with: "It's a decent trade-off: we ignore images of war because we're oversaturated by television, but *Deadwood* is a pretty awesome show."

Edward Said's *Orientalism*: Racist caricatures allow people to take over countries without thinking of those people as anything more than those caricatures. Get ready for the next great war between New York sketch artists and Jack Nicholson.[8]

---

8. Caricatures! Am I right? Like the people who draw the— You get it! It's a terrible joke! I should cut it from the book? Why didn't I cut it? Why am I writing this here and not deleting the bad joke? Oh well. I guess it's in the book now.

Poetry, or the "I Wish I Could Focus Enough to Appreciate This, but I'll Probably Read It While Pooping" Section

Poets are the only people who can make writing interesting, because the poems don't have to be long. But what they lack in breadth they make up for in the most flaccid of subjects. Keats looked at pots, Wordsworth looked at the same building over and over for his entire life, several poets wrote about a particular rock[9] or bird they had seen. Somewhere along the line, poets really went nuts and asked, since no one was reading their poems anyway, why not just make them as opaque as possible?

Finally, people laid some fat beats behind what is essentially Gerard Manley Hopkins's rhyme scheme (he wrote what sounded the most fun rather than making sure the words made sense to anyone—Jay-Z style). Rap, Spoken Word, and Hopkins led poetry back to the English-language peak that Shakespeare had previously set. Then, those who were influenced by these poets came up with slam poetry, making poetry the absolute worst kind of writing.

Poetry Subgenres

English Romanticism

Romantic poets wrote about how Nature and Time could really fuck you if you weren't careful. They also wrote that Greece was the coolest.

---

9. I'm not really sure what lapis lazuli is, but apparently it's impressive.

The Beat Poets
Pushing the envelope of how long you're willing to read super-repetitive envelope pushing.

Modernist Poets
Poets such as T. S. Eliot wrote purposefully hard-to-understand poems so readers could pretend they "get it" and look smart without ever understanding them. Bless this man for all his seemingly hard work.

Who You'll See in the Poetry Section

Bookstore staff who want to avoid patrons of the bookstore.

Books You'll Find in the Poetry Section

Sylvia Plath's *Collected Poems*: If you don't feel like writing your own suicide note, feel free to buy this and keep it near your bed for when you off yourself.

Emily Dickinson: See Sylvia Plath's *Collected Poems* description.

Gertrude Stein's *Tender Buttons*: If this book if this book if this book if should be read, it should be should be if only if only if only you're fifteen and high on paint fumes.

Derek Walcott's *Omeros*: A new version of *The Odyssey* that takes place in the Caribbean. The target demographic for this book is six people.

Children's, or the "I Vaguely Remember This from My Youth and Therefore Love It More Than I Love My Close Friends" Section

The only time the writers of children's literature stop laughing is when they arrive at the bank. They attend to their business of cashing million-dollar royalty checks for writing three and a half sentences, then go about their day of laughing uncontrollably and pressing the tips of their fingers together in a Zen-like meditation on how good it is to be rich.

How children's books are written: Writers pick a subject kids enjoy, like animals or trees. The writers then make three observations about those things (trees are big, animals act like humans sometimes, etc.), then repeat the same few words on every page. Extra points for rhyming words and hiring a great illustrator!

Who You'll See in the Children's Section

Children, dummy! And the world's saddest bookstore employee dressed in a Winnie-the-Pooh costume.

Books You'll Find in the Children's Section

Dr. Seuss books: Sometimes simple poems about animals, other times stories with overtones concerning abortion or the Cuban Missile Crisis. His real name was Theodor Geisel, a name that sounded too German at a time when Germans were not the best role models for children.

Books by Shel Silverstein: Not for children. A whole generation thought these would be good for their kids, and now look at us. We're all ironic assholes because we read *Uncle Shelby's ABZ Book* before reading the books it was making fun of. We're fucked.

Bestsellers, or the "I Can't Believe How Stupid People Are— Oh, Wait, This Book Looks Pretty Good" Section

Not all books are depressing ruminations on a previous era when real love and loss existed, nor are all books depressing ruminations on the Holocaust or depressing ruminations on sitting in a room being depressed. And not every book is a thicker-than-a-TV-chef's-waist biography of a former U.S. president. Some books are full of beautiful and intriguing stories about sex, murder, and wizards.

Who You'll See in the Bestsellers Section

Teenagers and college students who pretend to only like these books ironically, when in fact they genuinely enjoy them.[10]

Books You'll Find in the Bestsellers Section

The Harry Potter series: *My So-Called Life* but with more magic!

---

10. Own up to it, dorks!

Stephenie Meyer's *Twilight*: *My So-Called Life* with vampires!

The Girl with the Dragon Tattoo by Stieg Larsson: All the economic scandal of *Too Big to Fail*, but with twice as much rape!

Stephen King's *Carrie*: *My So Called Life* if the main character could kill people with her mind.

CHAPTER FIVE

On Titles

The proper way to judge a book is by quickly glancing at its cover. Usually, you can tell just how bad the book is by how much writing appears on the front. The whole point of book covers is to trick people into opening the book! Don't crowd the cover of your book with another book, books! Simplify. Make the title as short as possible. Many short titles, however, are inordinately cryptic or so vague you can't even finish reading the half sentence that describes the book.[1] Also, since most people never finish the books they buy, many books might be sending the wrong message to guests visiting your home library: What if you buy a book filled with all types of freaky sex but the title sounds tame?[2] And what if the title suggests something fun when

---

1. *Love in the Time of . . .* WHO CARES, TOO LONG! *Catch-22*? Looks like there's math in that book. No thank you!

2. Note to reader: John Updike's Rabbit books are not about rabbits.

in fact the inside is filled with mind-numbing moronic drivel?[3] You don't want people to think you're dumb for fake-liking the wrong books. So how can you pick?

Here are a few pieces of classic literature with better titles so you can choose the book that suits you best and start skimming the back cover for talking points. Like choosing a life partner, choosing a book should be done quickly and for the shallowest of reasons. You'll learn how to pretend to love it later. Once you've chosen the right book for you, I will teach you how to not read the book or (if you would like to waste precious hours of your life) help you finish the first and last book you'll ever read. These covers will sum up the contents of each book:

---

3. There are so many authors I could piss off in this footnote, but I can only choose one: Tucker Max. What a jerk.

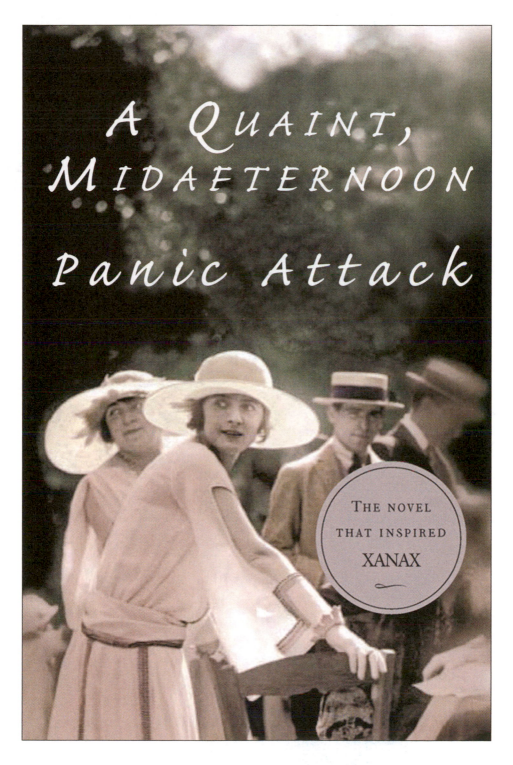

A Quaint, Midaeternoon Panic Attack

THE NOVEL
THAT INSPIRED
XANAX

Virginia Woolf: *Mrs. Dalloway*

EAT
UNTIL YOU
FEEL PRETTY
by Eric Carle

Eric Carle: *The Very Hungry Caterpillar*

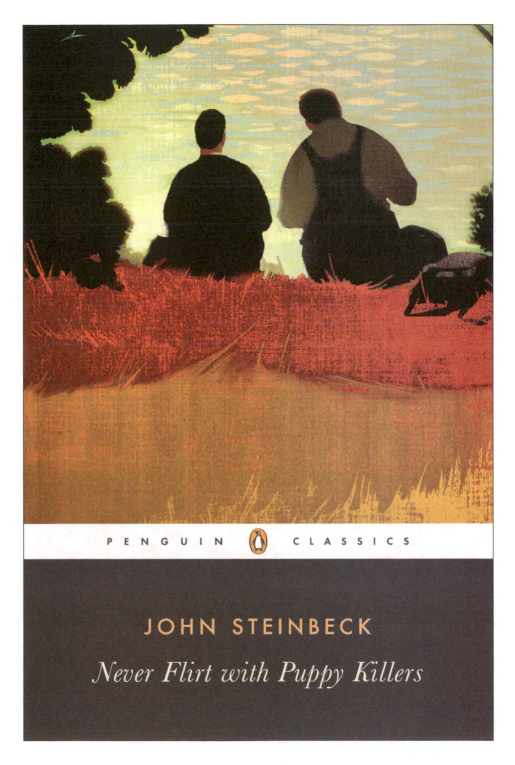

PENGUIN CLASSICS

JOHN STEINBECK

Never Flirt with Puppy Killers

John Steinbeck: *Of Mice and Men*

All Right! FINE, ASSHOLE!

Eleventh Edition

I Didn't Use the Word "Quixotic" Right!

AN ENCYCLOPÆDIA BRITANNICA® COMPANY

Merriam-Webster's Dictionary

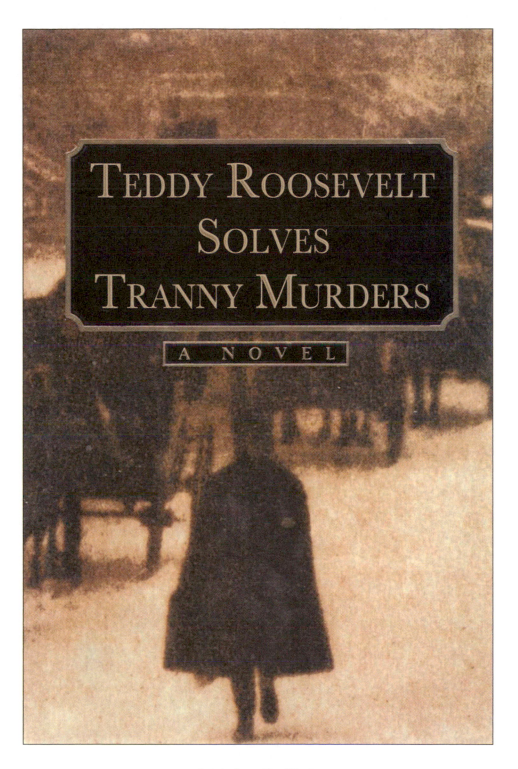

TEDDY ROOSEVELT
SOLVES
TRANNY MURDERS

A NOVEL

Caleb Carr: *The Alienist*

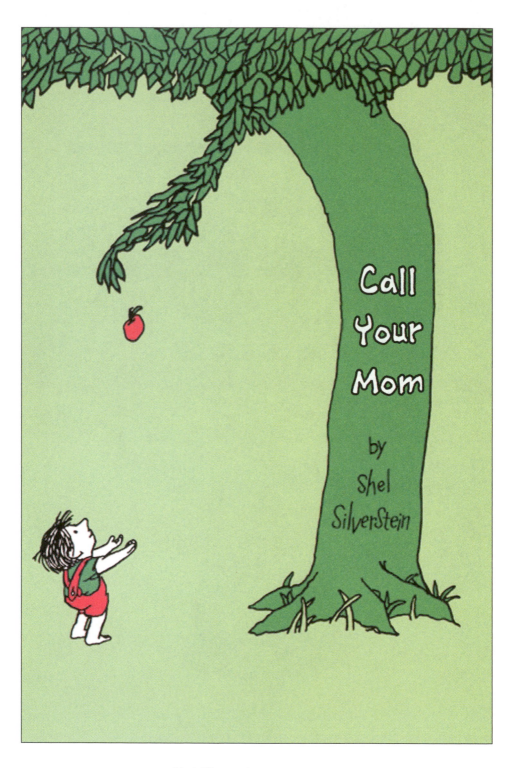

Call
Your
Mom

by
Shel
Silverstein

Shel Silverstein: *The Giving Tree*

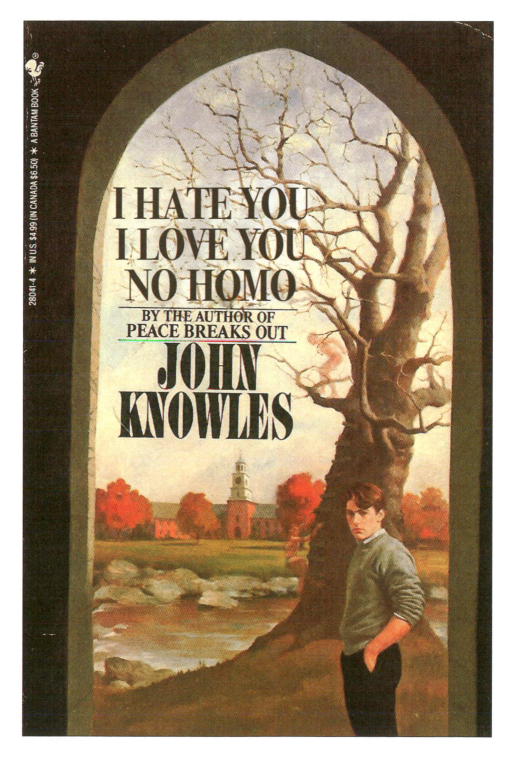

I HATE YOU
I LOVE YOU
NO HOMO

BY THE AUTHOR OF
PEACE BREAKS OUT

JOHN
KNOWLES

John Knowles: *A Separate Peace*

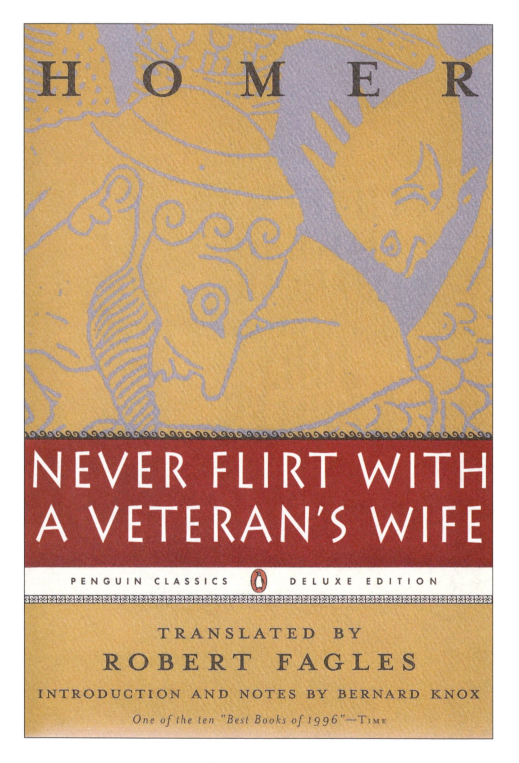

HOMER

NEVER FLIRT WITH
A VETERAN'S WIFE

PENGUIN CLASSICS   DELUXE EDITION

TRANSLATED BY
ROBERT FAGLES
INTRODUCTION AND NOTES BY BERNARD KNOX
One of the ten "Best Books of 1996" —Time

Homer: *The Odyssey*

F. Scott Fitzgerald: *The Great Gatsby*

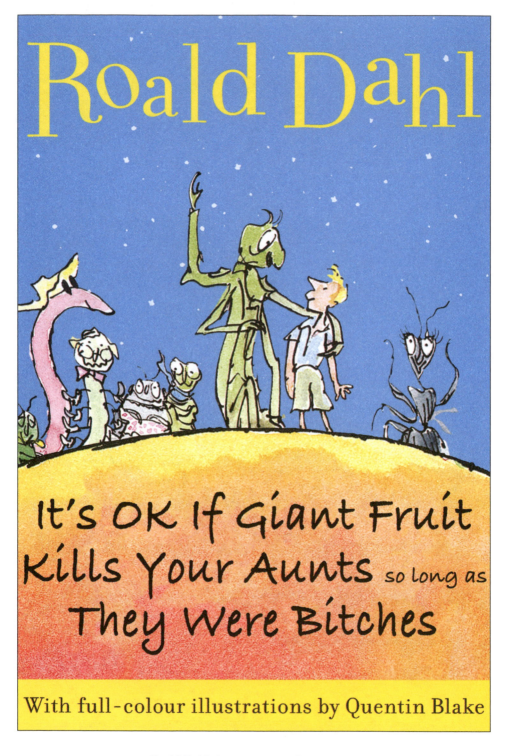

Roald Dahl: *James and the Giant Peach*

ONE LONG SENTENCE ABOUT HANDJOBS

BY

JAMES JOYCE

James Joyce: *Ulysses*

DADDY ISSUES AND A BAD BREAKUP FOUND ROME

VIRGIL

TRANSLATED BY
ROBERT FAGLES

INTRODUCTION BY BERNARD KNOX

PENGUIN CLASSICS · DELUXE EDITION

Virgil: *The Aeneid*

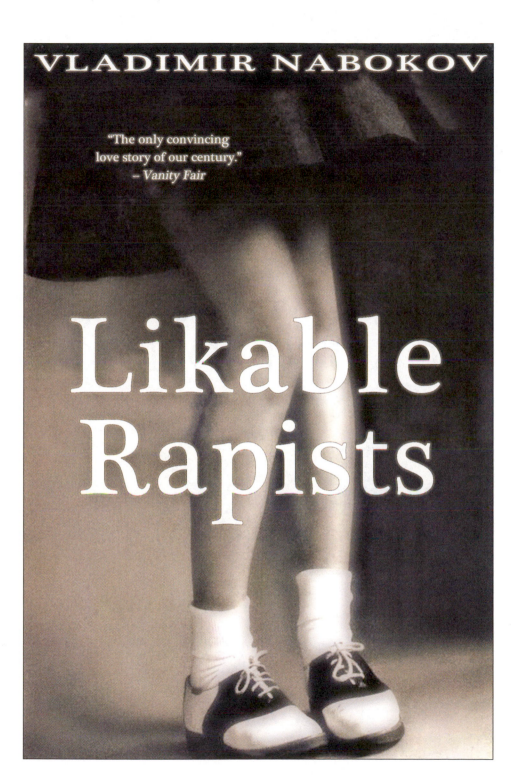

VLADIMIR NABOKOV

"The only convincing
love story of our century."
– *Vanity Fair*

Likable Rapists

Vladimir Nabokov: *Lolita*

I LOVE READING ABOUT POLITICS

ESPECIALLY WHEN MOST OF THE BOOK HAS NOTHING TO DO WITH POLITICS

FEATURING:
DRUNK
SOUTHERN
MEN
YELLING IN
LIBRARIES

Robert Penn Warren: *All the King's Men*

Anthony Burgess: *A Clockwork Orange*

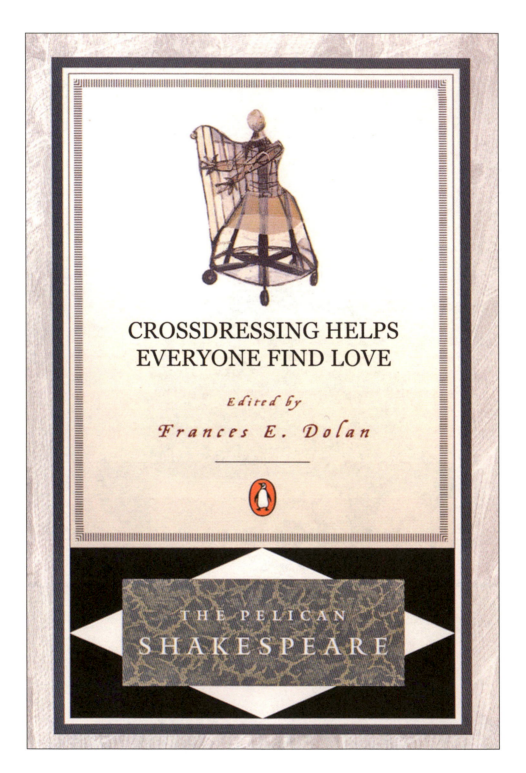

CROSSDRESSING HELPS
EVERYONE FIND LOVE

Edited by

Frances E. Dolan

THE PELICAN
SHAKESPEARE

William Shakespeare: *As You Like It* (and many other Shakespearean plays)

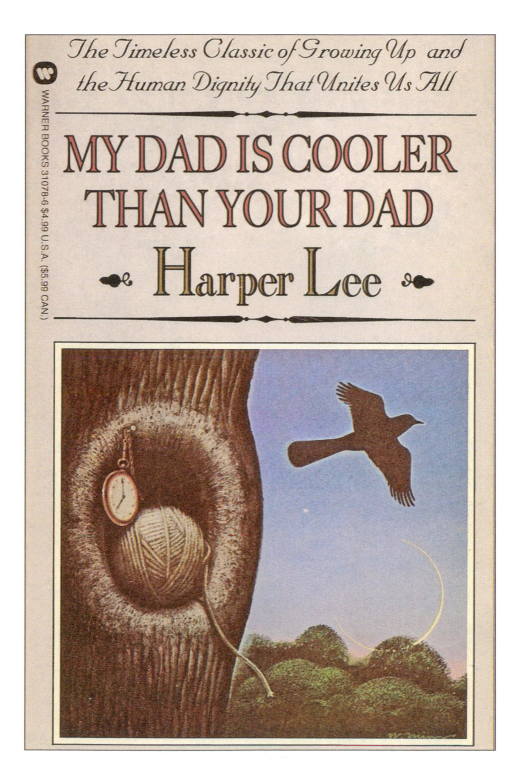

Harper Lee: *To Kill a Mockingbird*

Getting Fondled at
The County Fair

A New
Translation by
LYDIA
DAVIS

Gustave
Flaubert

Gustave Flaubert: *Madame Bovary*

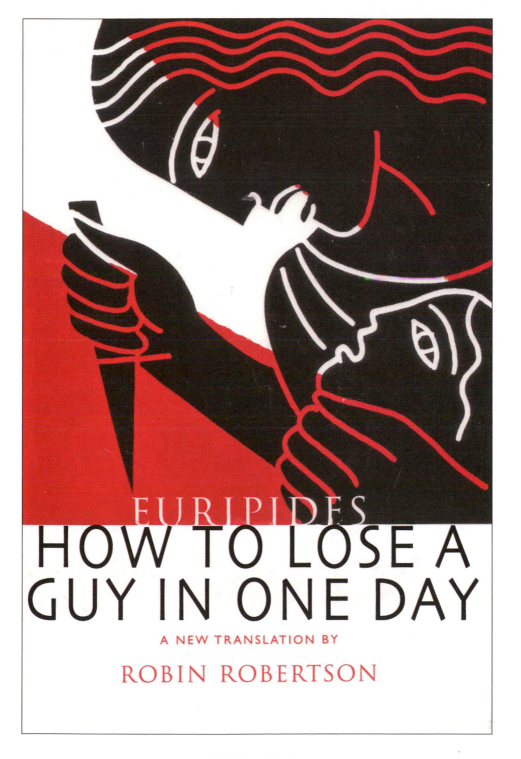

EURIPIDES

HOW TO LOSE A GUY IN ONE DAY

A NEW TRANSLATION BY

ROBIN ROBERTSON

Euripides: *Medea*

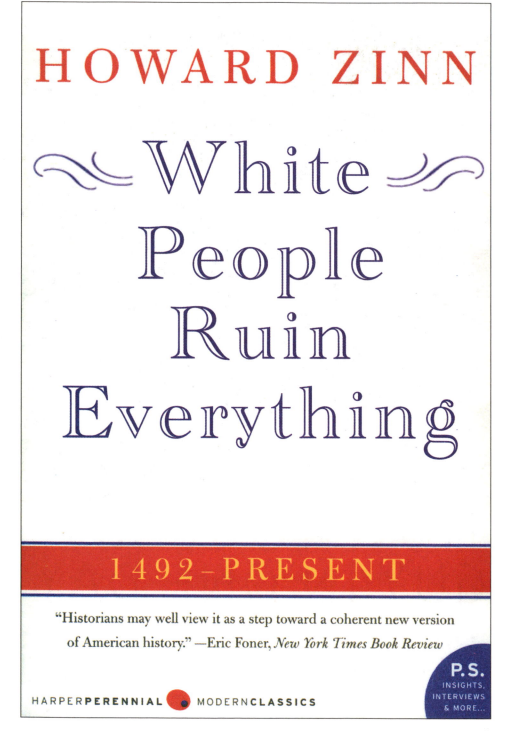

HOWARD ZINN

~ White ~

People

Ruin

Everything

1492–PRESENT

"Historians may well view it as a step toward a coherent new version
of American history." —Eric Foner, *New York Times Book Review*

HARPER**PERENNIAL** ● MODERN**CLASSICS**

P.S.
INSIGHTS,
INTERVIEWS
& MORE...

Howard Zinn: *A People's History of the United States*

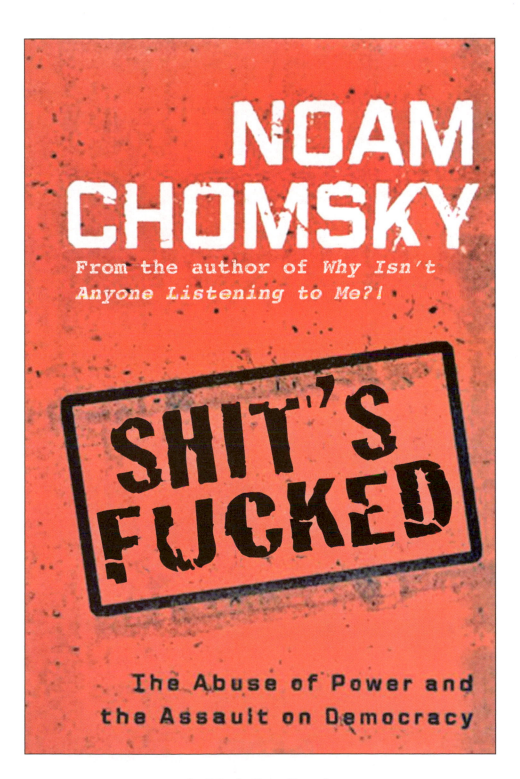

NOAM CHOMSKY

From the author of Why Isn't Anyone Listening to Me?!

SHIT'S FUCKED

The Abuse of Power and the Assault on Democracy

Anything by Noam Chomsky

Craig Thompson: *Blankets*

Maurice Sendak: *Where the Wild Things Are*

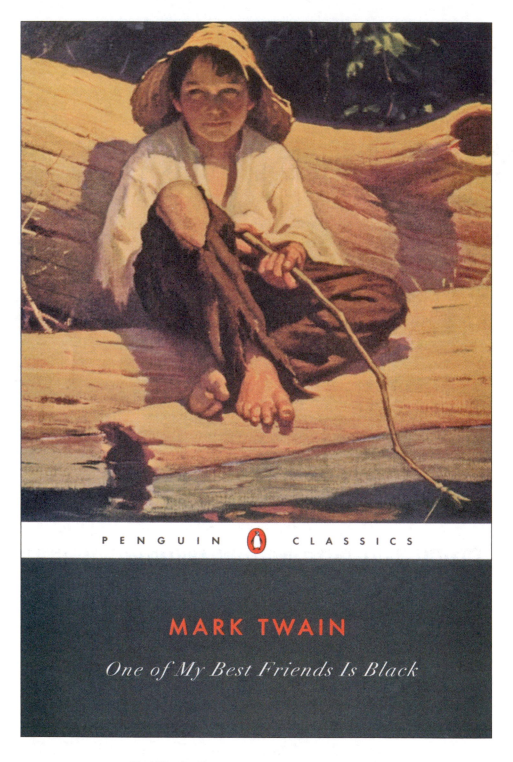

PENGUIN CLASSICS

MARK TWAIN

One of My Best Friends Is Black

Mark Twain: *The Adventures of Huckleberry Finn*

SUBMITTED BY MICHAEL AND DAVID MOLINA

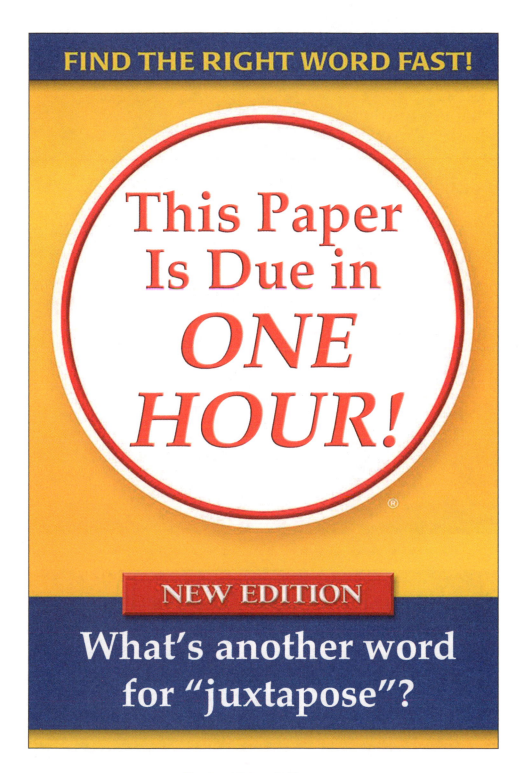

Merriam-Webster's Thesaurus

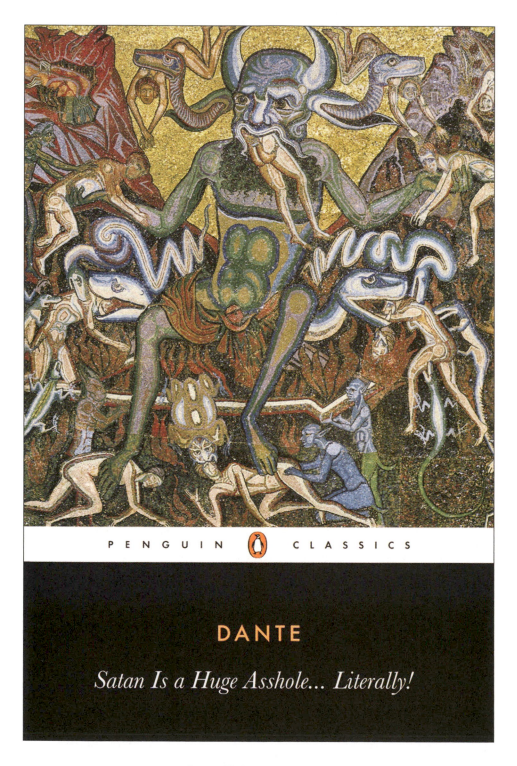

PENGUIN CLASSICS

DANTE

Satan Is a Huge Asshole... Literally!

Dante Alighieri: *The Inferno*

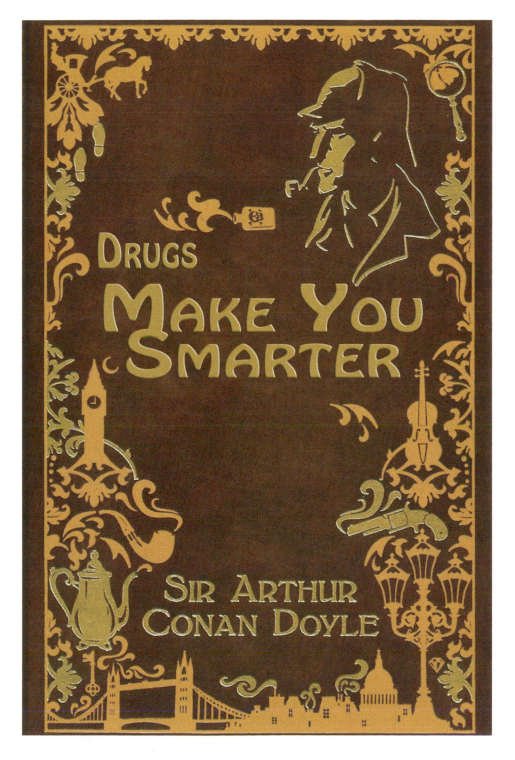

Sir Arthur Conan Doyle: *The Collected Stories of Sherlock Holmes*

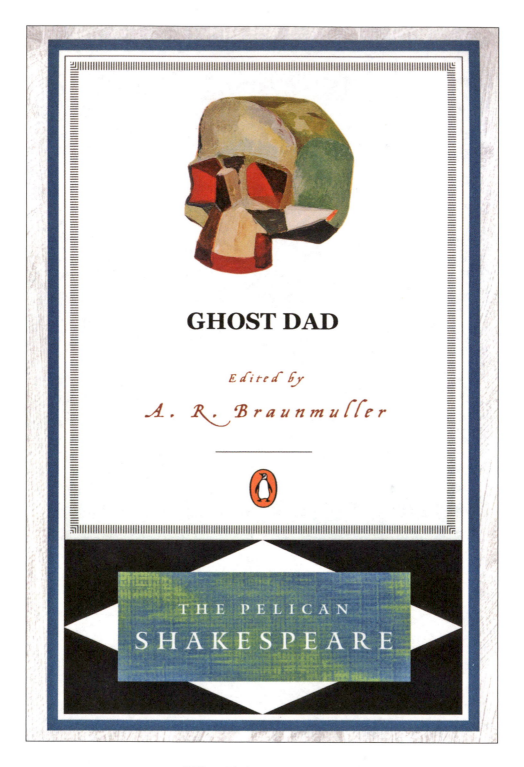

GHOST DAD

Edited by

A. R. Braunmuller

THE PELICAN
SHAKESPEARE

William Shakespeare: *Hamlet*

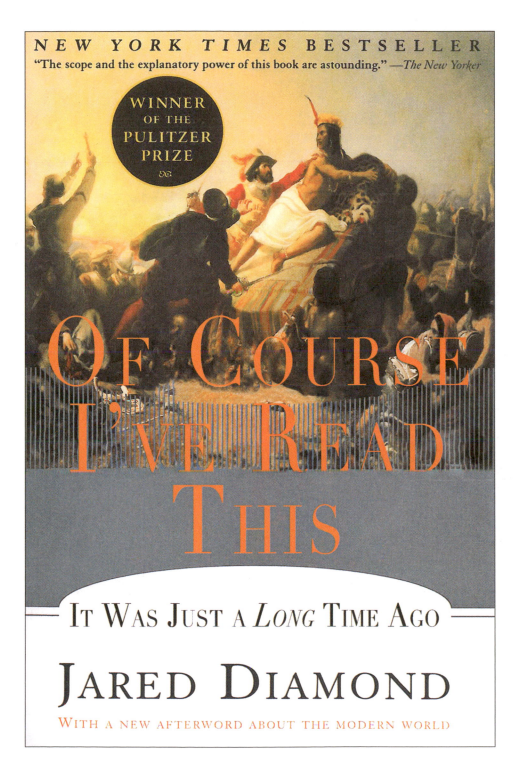

NEW YORK TIMES BESTSELLER

"The scope and the explanatory power of this book are astounding." —*The New Yorker*

WINNER
OF THE
PULITZER
PRIZE

OF COURSE
I'VE READ
THIS

— IT WAS JUST A *LONG* TIME AGO —

JARED DIAMOND

WITH A NEW AFTERWORD ABOUT THE MODERN WORLD

Jared Diamond: *Guns, Germs, and Steel*

The Last Story
Grandpa Told Us
Before We Sent
Him to the Home

Written by Judi Barrett
and Drawn by Ron Barrett

Judi Barrett and Ron Barrett: *Cloudy with a Chance of Meatballs*

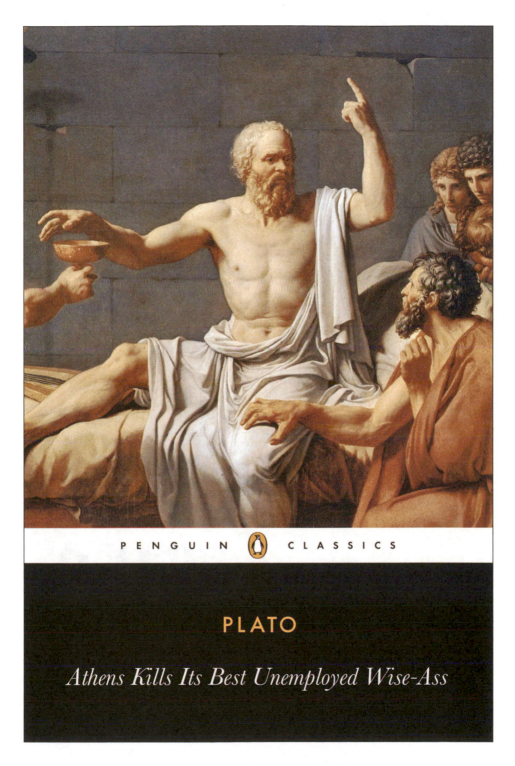

PENGUIN CLASSICS

PLATO

Athens Kills Its Best Unemployed Wise-Ass

Plato: *The Trial and Death of Socrates*

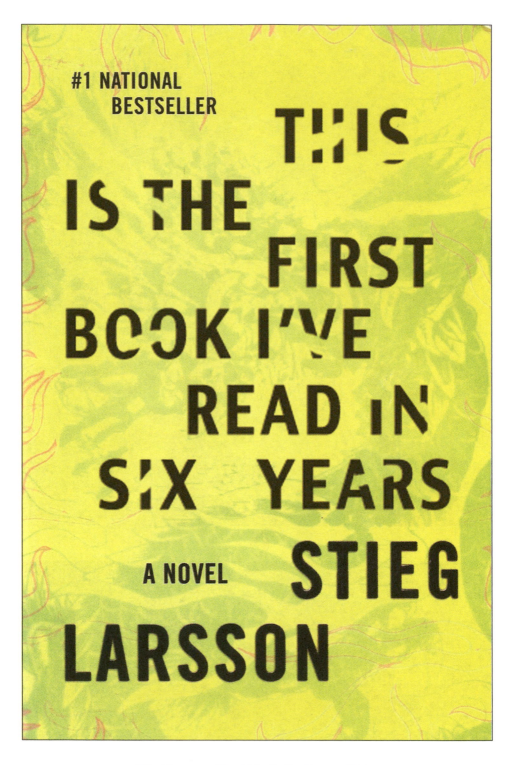

#1 NATIONAL
BESTSELLER

THIS
IS THE
FIRST
BOOK I'VE
READ IN
SIX YEARS
A NOVEL
STIEG
LARSSON

Stieg Larsson: *The Girl with the Dragon Tattoo*

CHAPTER SIX

How to Read

R eading can be hard if you don't know how to read. The best way to understand reading is by already knowing how to read. If you were not taught how to read, I will teach you now: Look at letters on paper, then form the letters into sounds, then comprehend the sounds as language. Language, of course, is the chosen method humans use to represent thoughts and label surroundings, objects, and people. By labeling people, places, and things we can warn like-minded humans where the dangerous ethnicities usually congregate.

If knowing how to read has yet to help you understand a book, don't fret. This section is devoted to those people who have attempted reading several words on multiple pages but failed to appreciate literature correctly. If that's you, here are some tips for becoming a better reader:

Step 1: Understand You're Reading Wrongly

Step one is all about acceptance. Books should not be read while relaxing on vacation or in common public reading spaces like coffee shops or strip clubs. Reading should be done at a desk with no one else around, and you should never talk to anyone about what the book makes you think.[1] Protect your thoughts and read in absolute silence in a tiny room with a single lightbulb or candle illuminating the otherwise empty space.

Step 2: Never Reread Anything

Books, especially novels, should be read as fast as your eyes can move. That way, you can know things faster. Nabokov said: "Curiously enough, one cannot read a book; one can only reread it." A great literary critic and writer thinks you must reread books to understand them. But you know what else Nabokov thought about all the time? Touching kids. Re-readers are child-touchers. Remember that.

Even if you do not fully comprehend what is happening in the book you're reading, keep going and don't look back. Your thoughts trump anyone else's, including the author's. If your mind wanders while you are reading, let it wander! Were you reading about a stoic character's stellar poker face and suddenly got reminded of the song "Poker Face" by Lady Gaga? Let your mind wander until you put the book down and start reading the song lyrics online. You just became more knowledge-able without forcing yourself to focus completely on one book.

Did you miss a whole chapter because you were thinking about a recent fight with someone? Are you imagining a fake fight that will most likely never happen because of your inability to stand up for yourself? Well, stew in it! What would you say to that jerk if he or she were

---

1. Beware of thought-theft! Advertisers are always mining new ideas in coffee shops; that's why sometimes you see a commercial and think, *That's just how my friends sound!* That's because people stole your friends' thoughts.

in the room with you right now? "NO! You shut your mouth! I clean my spoons when I'm done with them!" Whoa! While having that mental fight, you just blew through three pages of *Heart of Darkness* without worrying about what the book is about! That's three pages closer to the finish. Three pages closer to reaching your childhood dream of being one of those people who has read *Heart of Darkness*.

If this is the point where you're starting to ignore what I'm writing, I've provided a space to run your eyes over without the shame that comes with missing some crucial plot point or argument. Please enjoy the next minute or so by skimming this paragraph and thinking your own thoughts:

XXXXXXXXXXXXXXXXXXXXXXXXXXXXXXXXXXXXXXXXXXXXXXXXXXXXXXX
XXXXXXXXXXXXXXXXXXXXXXXXXXXXXXXXXXXXXXXXXXXXXXXXXXXXXXX
XXXXXXXXXXXXXXXXXXXXXXXXXXXXXXXXXXXXXXXXXXXXXXXXXXXXXXX
XXXXXXXXXXXXXXXXXXXXXXXXXXXXXXXXXXXXXXXXXXXXXXXXXXXXXXXX
XXXXXXXXXXXXXXXXXXXXXXXXXXXXXXXXXXXXXXXXXXXXXXXXXXXXXXX
XXXXXXXXXXXXXXXXXXXXXXXXXXXXXXXXXXXXXXXXXXXXXXXXXXXXXXXX
XXXXXXXXXXXXXXXXXXXXXXXXXXXXXXXXXXXXXXXXXXXXXXXXXXXXXXX
XXX XXXXXXXXXXXXXXXXXXXXXXXXXXXXXXXXXXXXXXXXXXXXXXXXXXXX
XXXXXXXXXXXXXXXXXXXXXXXXXXXXXXXXXXXXXXXXXXXXXXXXXXXXXXXX
XXXXXXXXXXXXXXXXXXXXXXXXXXXXXXXXXXXXXXXXXXXXXXX XXXXXX
XXXXXXXXXXXXXXXXXXXXXXXXXXXXXXXXXXXXXXXXXXXXXXXXXXXXXXX
XXXXXXXXXXXXXXXXXXXXXXXXXXXXXXXXXXXXXXXXXXXXXXXXXXXXXXX
XXXXXXXXXXXXXXXXXXXXXXXXXXXXXXXXXXXXXXXX XXXXXXXXXXXXXX
XXXXXXXXXXXXXXXXXXXXXXXXXXXXXXXXXXXXXXXXXXXXXXXXXXXXXXX
XXXXXXXXXXXXXXXXXXXXXXXXXXXXXXXXXXXXXXXXXXXXXXXXXXXXXXX
XXXXXXXXXXXXXXXXXXXXXXXXXXXXXXXXXXXXXXXXXXXXXXXXXXXXXXX
XXXXXXXXXXXXXXXXXXXXXXXXXXXXXXXXXXXXXXXXXXXXXXXXXXXXXXX
XXXXXXXXXXXXXXXXXXXXXXXXXXXXXXXXXXXXXXXXXXXXXXXXXXXXXXX
XXXXXXXXXXXXXXXXXXXXXXXXXXXXXXXXXXXXXXXXXXXXXXXXXXXXXXX
XXXXXXXXXXXXXXXXXXXXXXXXXXXXXXXXXXXXXXXXXXXXXXXXXXXXXXX
XXXXXXXXXXXXXXXXXXXXXXXXXXXXXXXXXXXXXXXXXXXXXXXXXXXXXXX

XXXXXXXXXXXXXXXXXXXXXXXXXXXXXXXXXXXXXXXXXXXXXXXXXXXXXX
XXXXXXXXXXXXXXXXXXXXXXXXXXXXXXXXXXXXXXXXXXXXXXXXXXXXXX
XXXXXXXXXXXXXXXXXXXXXXXXXXXXXXXXXXXXXXXXXXXXXXXXXXXXXX
XXXXXXXXXXXXXXXXXXXXXXXXXXXXXXXXXXXXXXXXXXXXXXXXXXXXXX
XXXX XXXXXXXXXXXXXXXXXXXXXXXXXXXXXXXXXXXXXXXXXXXXXXXXXX
XXXXXXXXXXXXXXXXXXXXXXXXXXXXXXXXXXXXXXXXXXXXXXXXXXXXXX
XXXXXXXXXXXXXXXXXXXXXXXXXXXXXXXXXXXXXXXXXXXXXXXXX XXXXX
XXXXXXXXXXXXXXXXXXXXXXXXXXXXXXXXXXXXXXXXXXXXXXXXXXXXXX
XXXXXXXXXXXXXXXXXXXXXXXXXXXXXXXXXXXXXXXXXXXXXXXXXXXXXX
XXXXXXXXXXXXXXXXXXXXXXXXXXXXXXXXXXXXXXXXXXXXXXXXXXXXXX
XXXXXXXXXXXXXXXXXXXXXXXXXXXXXXXXXXXXXXXXXXXXXXXXXXXXXX
XXXXXXXXXXXXXXXXXXXXXXXXXXXXXXXXXXXXXXXXXXXXXXXXXXXXXX
XXXXXXXXXXXXXXXXXXXXXXXXXXXXXXXXXXXXXXXXXXXXXXXXXXXXXX
XXXXXXXXXXXXXXXXXXXXXXXXXXXXXXXXXXXXXXXXXXXXXXXXXXXXXX
XXXXXXXXXXXXXXXXXXXXXXXXXXXXXXXXXXXXXXXXXXXXXXXXXXXXXX
XXXXXXXXXXXXXXXXXXXXXXXXXXXXXXXXXXXXXXXXXXXXXXXXXXXXXX
XXXXXXXXXXXXXXXXXXXXXXXXXXXXXXXXXXXXXXXXXXXXXXXXXXXXXX
XXXXXXXXXXXXXXXXXXXXXXXXXXXXXXXXXXXXXXXXXXXXXXXXXXXXXX
XXXXXXXXXXXXXX

WAKE UP! I hope you actually ran your eyes over the last page. There is a secret message inside for the incredibly astute reader.[2]

Step 3: Never Take Notes

What are you doing! Stop writing. STOP. Enjoying a book means letting it flow over you the exact way the author wrote it: in one sitting, while thinking about anything that popped into the old noggin, and without

---

2. Do you see it now? No? Look again. HA! See it now? That's right! America never landed on the moon.

some silly legal pad cluttering up his or her desk space. Reading is about reading, not writing. If you really want to remember something from a book later, just Google it. Or guess. That's how new, important thoughts are born.

Step 4: Imagine Someone Else Is Reading to You

You know who can imitate a great British accent? The inside of your head. Every time you're reading Shakespeare you'd better have Sir Ian McKellan's voice blasting inside your brain stadium. Another good person to use is comedian Gilbert Gottfried for anything too long, like Dickens. Then, reading a book is as relaxing as being read to, like when your mom read to you just before bed except now your mom is Gilbert Gottfried, which is much more fun/terrifying!

SOME LITERARY TERMS YOU SHOULD
KNOW BEFORE READING

In order to sound like you read all the time, you should lie not only about what you're reading but also about how and why you enjoy the book. Reading for the sake of reading is like attending a $1,000-a-plate fund-raising dinner just for the free breadsticks, instead of going because you want to legalize heroin. You read to have the upper hand in a conversation or political arena. To do that, you need to know how to talk.

Here are a few terms to practice. Insert any of these terms into the following quote and enjoy the attention of every person wearing glasses: "I loved the _____ in this book. It gave it the je ne sais quoi the author always manages to capture. Now let's have sex."

Allusion: A reference to a book that is not the book you're currently reading. Seriously! How is anyone supposed to start reading books when they're full of stuff from other books you haven't read. Sounds like a catch-22 to me.[3]

Allegory: A symbolic story usually with a moral like "Don't Shit Where Ya Eat" which Aesop tackled in his story "How the Kangaroo Got Dysentery."

Deus ex machina: Greek tragedies often ended by introducing a god in the last scene to wrap everything up. At the end of *Seven*, if Brad Pitt had opened "the box" and a clown popped out and made everyone laugh at the whole series of events, then "Yakety Sax" played and the credits rolled, that would be a great deus ex machina.

Irony: When something happens that you didn't expect but sort of thought would happen all along. Wait—hold on . . . It's like writing a book about terms like "irony" but not being able to find the words to describe irony. Wait, that's not it either, really. It's like buying this book for a friend and they like everything in it except this paragraph (admittedly shitty), so the friend re-gifts the book to someone he thinks would love this paragraph, but that friend re-gifts it to the original giver of the book, who sees all the names written on the inside cover of the book and suddenly hates everyone, including me, when the purpose of this book was to bring people together by not reading more. Confused? Me too.

Apostrophe: Directly addressing something that is either not present or so abstract no person would ever expect a response from it. When a crazy person sitting next to you on the bus yells, "O CAMPBELL'S SOUP

---

3. What's that? . . . Are you serious? Come on. Yes, you have. You could have never even heard of that book and still know what the phrase means. You could have not even heard about World War II and still understand that phrase. Fine. FINE! You're right! I'll never reference any other book without explaining exactly what I'm referencing even though this whole book is about other books. This book is going to look like a literary Escher painting . . . What?! GET OUT!

CAN! You KNOW I love you!" that's an example of apostrophe. Writers usually class it up by talking to the moon, which is equally crazy.

Byronic Hero: A main character with a slew of flaws whose main concern is overindulgence. Picture a really fat guy who likes doing really fat-guy things like getting Dorito powder stuck in his phone while texting someone to find out what song is in his head, instead of leaning over and opening his computer to find out.[4]

Mimesis: Representation or imitation. In *The Wire*, when everything in Baltimore is just as fucked as real-life Baltimore.

Catharsis: "Cleansing" action. When one character feels exonerated or gains a sense of accomplishment from completing a long-awaited task. Examples: When Hamlet kills Claudius, or when you finally remove a stringy piece of steak from between your teeth.

Hamartia: A tragic flaw. Usually leads to the downfall of the main character. Mine is herpes—errr, lechery!

Purple Prose: Flowery fantastical language that flows from the page with radiant resonance. What many professorial types would call "corny-ass shit."

Metonymy: An image strongly related to a person, place, or thing that represents that person, place, or thing: Ron Jeremy represents American virility and the sexual abilities all American males are born with.

Synecdoche: An image that is part of the whole and represents the whole. Ron Jeremy's actual penis represents Ron Jeremy. Also his mustache.

Hyperbole: Exaggeration. Whenever my grandfather told me I'd never amount to anything, that was hyperbole.[5] Good thing I took it with a grain of salt since he was 864 years old.

---

4. I do that. I'm writing about me.

5. Though he was not that far off.

Simile: Using "like" or "as" to compare a subject to something else. Here is a hyperbole/simile: "Getting my flu shot felt like getting shot with a gun, only times, like, a million."

Metaphor: Comparing two things without "like" or "as." "This is my body." Jesus Christ, using a metaphor at the most confusing moment. Led to the creation of the more austere Protestant Church that, while having a slightly boring appearance, understands the definition of metaphor.

Denouement: The part of the book, post-climax, that wraps everything up. Unnecessary excess at the end of a story. The foreskin of literature.

Foil: A character made to play off another character's quirks. Joey to Phoebe. Jesus to Satan. Laser Pointer to Cat.

Double entendre: A word or sentence with two or more different meanings. Usually dirty, funny, or extremely poignant and political. Many writers follow up these sentences with "that's what she said," as in John Donne's famous poem "The Flea": "It suck'd me first, and now sucks thee / that's what she said! . . . Hast thou since / Purpled thy nail in blood of innocence? / If you know what I mean . . ." A more collegiate term is "De-familiarization," which means making sex and boners sound like other activities or objects. "The bow of the vessel was turned up and the sail was an erect staff as it entered the port . . ." (you get the picture).

In medias res: Starting in the middle of the action. The best books are written this way, so people aren't bogged down with reading about who is who and what is where before the action starts. Vonnegut said, "Start as close to the end as possible." A really great book would go like this: "Then everyone died. The End." Succinct and gripping.

CHAPTER SEVEN

How to Talk to Others About Books

Now that you are carrying around a book everywhere, people are going to start asking questions. You must prove yourself regardless of whether or not you've read or even started to read your first book.

A lot of folks in the world want you to think you're dumb so they can privatize Social Security, bankrupt it, and point the finger at you for the stock market crash because you were not being the good consumer you're supposed to be. But you're smart. You should be able to tell these cash-addicted, emotionless cyborgs that you're not going to take it anymore! But first, you'll need to look smart and act your way through some tricky situations so these cyborgs think you're one of them.

Though most people do not read for leisure, powerful people pretend reading is all they do. Here's a crash course in surviving in the literary community.

How to Pretend You've Read a Book

We've all done it. Everyone is talking about *Mockingjay* (a children's book that probably takes about an hour to read), but you accidentally read *To Kill a Mockingbird* (like an adult), and now you're stuck in a conversation with no way out! Here are a few helpful hints to prove you've read a book you've never opened:

1. Be the First to Bring Up Other Books

Everyone's talking about Stieg Larsson, but you've got a trump card: knowledge of other books that no living person has ever read. When there's a lull, say: "It reminds me of those great pieces of dialogue in *Double Indemnity* (the book not the film, of course!)— What? You've never read that? Well then I'll spare you my comparison of Larsson's work to *The Bonfire of the Vanities*. Well, it's a good book, too. You should read more!"

2. Listen and Respond

If the book everyone is discussing has to do with some relevant cause or current political movement, bring up "facts" you learned from reading the *New York Times* (or watching Rachel Maddow tell you about the *New York Times*). Here's a good fact you can use to deflect questions about a book: "Did you know ninety percent of our tax money is spent on war stuff? Even when you buy cookies, the friendliest food! It really makes you think." If you can extemporize on the Middle East, everyone who read *The Kite Runner* will feel their own knowledge is tawdry in comparison.

3. Bring Up Travel

One way to make aloof people feel shame for wasting their youth is to bring up all the places you've been that they haven't. Even if you've never been anywhere, start speaking about the "Russian People" as if you lived in St. Petersburg for the first half of your life. Make up facts about places: "The last time I was in Paris, I noticed more and more people wearing cardigans, so what you're saying about the book makes perfect sense," or "Yes, the Japanese do love snow cones!" Did anyone ask you if you read the book they're discussing? Nope. It's all about you and your travels. Say your dad was in the Air Force, so moving around the world was kind of boring to you.

4. Start a Book Club

This might seem backward, but think about how much leeway people will give if you're the person organizing a social event. People will think you love reading when really you just like hanging out with your friends. You think Oprah had enough time to read all those books she put an Oprah's Book Club sticker on? Well . . . she probably did. She has nearly all the money and therefore all of the time, but: Do you think anyone would mind if she didn't get around to reading one or two of those books? Heck no! She was too busy hosting her show and negotiating her contract to purchase the moon.

Here's how it can work for you: go online and look for smart books by smart people, make a list, and gather all your friends to discuss one of those books each week. As soon as it's your turn to speak, say, "I liked it overall, but the protag— OH! I forgot about my cookies!" Then go to the kitchen and bring out warm chocolate chip cookies. Who's the best? You are.

For a book club guide, see Appendix B.

5. Adopt the Cowboy-with-a-Past Style

Pretend the book being discussed brings up bad memories or a terrible time in your life. The next time someone brings up *War and Peace*, tell people you loved it, but allude to a darker time that interfered with (and yet, somehow, made more poignant) your understanding of Tolstoy's great novel. Maybe a breakup, or a scary drug experience, or a depressing vacation with the few surviving members of your broken family. Don't give too many details, but sigh occasionally and stare into the distance, as if the memory of the book is located somewhere on the horizon, where a piece of your soul is also hidden. You're the coolest. You should write a book!

TRANSLATIONS FOR COMMONLY USED PHRASES CONCERNING BOOKS

Whether you're stuck at an airport with a stranger or in prison for murder one, eventually people will tell you their thoughts on books. If it seems everyone else enjoys books more than you do, here are a few translations of platitudes that may prove revealing:

When someone says . . .	It really means . . .
"I read that book, but it was a long time ago."	"I never read that book."
"My teacher ruined that book for me."	"I never read that book."
"I liked it. It really flowed."	"I never read that book, or anything else for that matter."
"I appreciate the book, but I don't love it."	"I did not finish reading that book, and all my friends were really mean to me when I said I didn't like it."

"I hate that book."	"I read that book in its entirety because a girl I am no longer dating told me I had to read it," or "I never read that book because it was required reading for school and school sucks."
"A daring, expansive portrayal of the South."	"This is a longwinded book about three generations of racists."
"This book is pushing a pro-gay agenda on my son."	"I think I might be gay."
"This is a very important book. You should really read it."	"I remember six or seven words from that Malcolm Gladwell book, so you should read it because three or four of the words you were saying were also in that book. What were the words? Ummm. Genius, choice, mind. Yeah, you'll love it. Right up your alley."
"I see why you liked this book."	"You're a stupid person."
"It's not my cup of tea."	"I don't like anything, especially books."
"I've been meaning to read that!"	"I've have no idea what you're talking about."
"This book made me cry!"	"I have emotions! It makes me better than other people. What's that? Well, no, I didn't cry-cry. My eyes sorta watered while I was reading."
"I love this book!"	"This is the first book I've finished since college."

Venn Diagram

People who love books vs.
People who hate other people

How to Pretend You've Read a Specific Book

Sometimes, just saying a few words about a text can make you sound smarter than those who can expound upon it for hours. For "brevity is the soul of wit . . ." See? I've never even read *Harry Potter*, but people think I'm smart just because I can quote it. The following are words and phrases you can say when a particular book is brought up that you claim you've read:

The Iliad: "How about those spears? It's like they hit every body part during books thirteen to fifteen!"

Midnight's Children: "Which would you rather have: telepathy or the ability to smell things from far away? Smell, huh? But what about poop? You'd want to smell poop from far away? I guess you're right. Smelling poop is better than hearing everyone's disgusting boner-thoughts."

Hard Times: "Those were some pretty hard times! Am I right?"

Lolita: "Did you know Nabokov was an entomologist? Weird, huh?"

Frankenstein: "No, actually, it's I-gor! Ha! Right, guys?"

Don Quixote: "Windmills, crazy!"

Robinson Crusoe: "What would I bring on a desert island? Slaves. Definitely slaves for me."

Catch-22: "You've never read *Catch-22*!?! You're missing out!"

WHAT AUTHOR ARE WE TALKING ABOUT?
A TAXONOMICAL KEY

Have you ever been reading a book that did not include a header with the author's name or book title at the top of each page (how confounding!)? Have you ever entered partway through a literary conversation and had no idea which book your friends are speaking about? Before you go through the excruciating task of flipping all the way to the cover, or (heaven forfend!) ask your friends what book they're talking about (like an idiot!), use this handy identifier:

1. Was the book published after the year 1900? If yes, go to question 2. If no, go to question 1(a).

1(a). Are you serious? How old is that book? Like a million years old? Can you even understand what the characters are talking about or is it all in some old-timey "thee and thou" speak?? PUT IT DOWN! It is not worth knowing more about.

2. Is there a lot of sex in it? If yes, go to question 3. If no, go to question 2(a).

2(a). Why bother? Not even one scene? You might as well read the dictionary.[1] If there's no sex involved but somehow the work still seems intriguing, go to 7.

3. Is it masturbation or sex with other people? Sex with other people, go to question 4. If masturbation, go to question 3(a).

3(a). *Portnoy's Complaint* by Philip Roth.

4. Is the sex awesome, guilt-free, and dirty, or do people feel really weird about it? If it's fun, go to 5. If characters feel weird about it, go to 4(a).

4(a). If the book is set in America, it's Dave Eggers, or if the sexual feelings are weird and the main character is a girl, it's Judy Blume. If it's in Mexico or Europe, go to 4(b).

4(b). Europe: Graham Greene, *The End of the Affair*. If Mexico, go to 4(c).

4(c). Mexico: Graham Green, *The Power and the Glory*.

5. Is the book set in America or abroad? For America, go to question 6. For abroad go to question 5(a).

5(a). If it's in a Spanish-speaking country, it's Gabriel García Márquez. If not, go to 5(b).

5(b). If it's in France it's Henry Miller. If not, go to 5(c).

5(c). If in Prague, it's Milan Kundera. If not, go to 5(d).

5(d). If it's Ireland, it's James Joyce. If not, go to 5(e).

5(e). Name a country, think about a writer from that country . . . If the

---

1. The word "sex" is in this book, by the way. Sometimes with pictures!

writer's books are popular enough that you've heard of that writer, then he or she definitely writes about sex.

6. John Updike, Norman Mailer, or just guess a name you've heard from school. If no one has read the author you bring up, you're the smartest person in the room regardless.

7. Possibly talking about *Toy Story 3*.[2]

_____
2. Not a book.

What to Do Now That You've Read Your First Book: Literary Insults

You did it! You finished (or are pretending to have finished) a book. Congratulations! Your work, however, is not done. Book nerds will soon test you by condescendingly asking about your new favorite (only) book you've read. Well, I say these weak-armed half-witted obvi-virgins have pushed us around long enough! Now that you're feeling the pain-resistant, heroin-like hubris that accompanies finishing a book, it's time to start treating lesser people like the sad saps they are. You can rely on the classic insults: "four eyes," "dweeb," and "clearly-repressed-boy-who-I-would-be-friends-with-if-it-weren't-for-my-inability-to-accept-difference-n00b." But since you've just read a great book, it's time to put those esoteric references to good use. Here are some literary lacerations that will make you sound as smart as possible and take these pricks down a peg. Commence the nerd roast!

"Last time I saw a mouth that big, it was dragging Captain Ahab to his watery grave!"

"I haven't seen a face this ugly since Perseus killed the Kraken!"

"The only thing sadder than you is a Joycean epiphany!"

"You're as weak as a passive sentence written in negative form. And probably not considered by anyone to be worth more than an adverb."

"Is your Dewey Decimal number in the 521s? Because you're fat enough to be listed under 'celestial mechanics.'"

"Last time I talked to someone this brain-dead, he was walking out of Room 101."

"If ignorance is strength, then you must be going after the 'strongest person in the world' award!"

"Last time I saw someone this brain-dead, I pity-smothered him with a pillow and escaped the psych ward."

"The only person who would enjoy being near you is Oedipus. He's blind and only hangs out with the inbred."

"Yo Mama so fat when Atlas shrugged, it was so she would fall off."

"Hey, Harold Bloom called. He cited a number of Shakespeare quotes that describe you, including: 'a wretch whose natural gifts are poor,' 'thou bloodier villain than terms can give thee out,' and 'cock-face.'"

"Last time I saw a guy this ugly, he was calling on his father Poseidon to punish Odysseus."

"Why don't you make like a Tolstoy character, and kill yourself?"

"When your mom was pregnant with you, she said she would treat it like the best Coleridge poem: She was going to end it prematurely while on opium."

"If my dog were as ugly as you, I'd bury it in a magical cemetery and wait for it to come back to life and kill me. That's how ugly you are. Just seeing you makes me want to die by the fangs of a ghost-dog."

CHAPTER EIGHT

Writing Your Own Book

Being a writer is fun if you never write anything yourself.[1] Otherwise, it's torture.[2] If you'd still like to write your own work, though, there are a few things you should know: Firstly, you will fail. Secondly, I'm serious. Give up. Give up now. You are not special. You have nothing interesting to tell the world. You are nothing. NOTHING, you sad bastard! I wouldn't read your book if I were in a Twilight Zone–esque library and I had nothing but time and a pair of unbroken glasses.

Are you still reading? Now that we've weeded out the dilettantes, here's what you should really know about writing professionally: Firstly,

---

1. You speak at bookstores and colleges, and the only writing you have to do is sign your own name and answer questions from audience members by essentially repeating their comment or question back to them! Preschoolers could do it!

2. Side effects include diabetes, self-loathing, and constant hiding behind book deadline to avoid all social commitments.

you will fail. Several times. Secondly, you will want to give up because you feel like you're not special and have nothing interesting to tell the world. So, if you must write, here are some facts to keep in mind as you get closer to federally assisted living and spiritual ruin.

Why People Write

The important thing to keep in mind while writing is why writers write. Writers write so they can have sex with many different people. The reason great writers often write about sex is because they're trying to slip the words "I'd have sex with you" into every reader's mind, and those sleaze-buckets would have sex with any of those readers! This is not subliminal. Most writers are very up-front about wanting to have sex with everyone on the planet.[3]

Another reason to write is because all writers are self-hating masochists. Writers love sitting in a room alone, pondering their motives for all the shameful shit they've done in years past and putting it down on paper in the simplest, most unforgiving prose. Writers are in charge of cataloging the worst issues of the human condition. They're like journalists who only report on awful feelings. Most people try to forget their venal sins by actively living their lives and becoming better people, but writers choose to sit at a desk and mentally flagellate themselves for things that weren't as bad as they think. The result is a great book or a suicide or both!

Lastly, writers write to make millions upon millions of dollars by selling books that three years later will be worth a penny each.

---

3. I would, too! Visit http://imseriouslynotkidding.tumblr.com.

How Writers Write

If there's one thing writers have in common it's the ability to spend a lot of time not writing. Whether they're drinking at a bar with friends, drinking at home, or having a drink at the office from their desk-drawer Glenlivet bottle at 8 a.m., writers have managed to find a slew of ways to avoid writing.

What does this mean for you? Well, if you're a chain-smoking alcoholic philanderer, you're one ticket to a bullfight away from becoming a great author.[4] If you're a green-tea-and-kombucha-drinking, bird-watching, *Radiolab*-listening, socially liberal, 6:30 a.m. jogging, crossword-finishing, American dream–achieving, happily married freak, there's still a chance for you to publish a great book, but you need discipline. The best way to write is to be famous enough[5] that a publisher hires someone else to write your book for you. Short of that, here are the only ways to write an entire book:

Never Leave Your House: Your Book Is Now Your Baby

And just like a baby, you need to feed it constantly and shake it awake at any moment. Your book must become a heavy burden that you never let yourself be distracted from. Did the phone just ring? Ignore it. Bills to pay? Ignore them. Feel like you're getting chubby? Ignore your weak body! The power of the mind is all that matters! Getting fatter just means your brain will get bigger, and that will lead to more brilliant writing. You must think and worry about your book constantly or it

---

4. Or if you're English, "one physical deformity away"; Irish, "one self-exile away."

5. Or to have had sex with someone famous enough.

will be terrible. Never go outside or walk. The Sun will steal your thoughts. Give up all hobbies. Don't speak to your family. Your book is your only family now.

Set Aside Time, Each and Every Day, to Sob into a Pillow

Life in general is really tough, and now that you're staring at a blank page that seems to whisper "Go back to grad school and study Actuarial Science," life's even tougher. The page is like a disapproving parent who wants you to do something "more productive with your time." And just like an old parental lion, that page must be fought to the death and replaced by a page of your words! You are the one in charge here!

Achieving this goal has a high emotional cost. To relieve the pain, each day have a good, screaming cry for at least twenty minutes, or punch something repeatedly.

Try Not to Sleep

Have you ever been up so late you start laughing uncontrollably or crying from frustration and sleep deprivation? This is your body telling you you're in the prime writing space! Think of how vulnerable and open you are. You can't even think, let alone feel awkward, about what you're writing. Just put it all out there. That's it. You're in the zone. The writing zone. Now all that stuff about your parents and what you wish you were eating and how you wish you could sleep more will be laid out on the page, unedited by a cynical, well-nourished brain. Did you know most people do not sleep enough or eat healthy foods? Now you can relate because you're an unhealthy angry person who looks ten years older than your actual age.

Write While Drinking

Some writers have trouble focusing because writing can be as tedious as watching baseball.[6] Luckily, we have a medicine that has helped us pay attention for thousands of years without feeling like our brains were about to curl in on themselves and commit brainicide. That medicine is alcohol. Alcohol not only lets you feel like you're having an adventure while sitting at a desk, but, should you drink enough, it precludes you from leaving the house. Also, you won't feel like talking to anyone while hungover. That makes for a lot of writing time!

Never Read Anyone Else's Writing

Writing is about writing, not reading! You're the authority on what others should read: your writing. The only book you should ever read is your own book. If you start reading another person's book, suddenly your fingers will start moving on the keyboard, uncontrollably rewriting books that have already been written. Once the disease of another author's influence is inside you, you can never get it out. Now you're a plagiarist! Tsk, tsk. Good thing most people never read more than one book.

---

6. I said it!

UNDERSTANDING THE WRITING PROCESS

Before I started writing this book, I used to constantly say to myself: "I'm a genius and no one will let me prove it!" Now that I have a deadline to finish this book, I've realized: "Wow. I'm fucking dumb!" Here's the difference between how you think you'll write, and how you'll actually write:

How You Should Write	How You Will Write
As soon as you have an idea, get to work on it right away!	Congratulate yourself on finally coming up with a good idea by drinking a beer.
Organize your thoughts.	Write a sentence, celebrate by eating.
Complete an entire section (get it all on paper!).	Complain to a friend about writing. Eat all remaining food in the house.
Realize that though you're not the most brilliant writer, your hard work has given you perspective on how your literary heroes must have spent years working before anything good came out.	Feel a surge of encouragement! Sit down to write— Hey! A rerun of *Glee* is on. Watch it!
Stay disciplined.	Check Facebook.
After editing for a year, finish great novel.	Let editor edit your terrible book into something publishable.
Die just before publication to boost sales.	Live a long, healthy life as a professor of Humanities.

Books from the Outside In

Making Sure You Can Sell It Before You Take the Time to Write It

In preparation for no one reading your book but still taking the time to buy it, you need to make the outside of your book as buyable as possible. People browse books the same way they browse gardening and musical equipment: They picture a beautiful day with hours of leisure time to hone their skills, then buy stuff, spend an hour with it, and quit. This is your target audience. The best way to get these people to purchase your book rather than some other schmuck's is to make the outside an object that makes each buyer feel better about his or her existence. Then fill the inside with a story that's been written a million times. No one will notice because he or she will most likely not finish the book. On the off chance people do read your book, they will have spent so much time invested in your writing that they'll have to give it a positive review lest they admit they wasted months reading a terrible, derivative book.

How to Title Your Book

Everyone knows covers sell books (just ask anyone who has made a living writing books about how to get books published). But you don't want to sound like an idiot, so here are a few tips on generating some unpretentious titles for your book:

1. **Go Big or Go Home.** Your title needs to be relevant and evocative! Go on Twitter and see what's "trending." Now incorporate that into your title. *Why She a Ho* and *You Know He a Freak If* and *Bieber Fever!* are all great ideas for titles. I know your book is about the correct ways to finish the wooden chairs on your deck,

but call it *Decked Out with Justin Bieber!* and you'll be swimming in cash money, honey!

2. **Great Writers Steal.** One thing I've learned from my six seconds in publishing is that titles are not copyrightable. Do you know what that means? It means pick your favorite book or movie and title your book after it! If you write a cookbook, call it *Apocalypse Now* or Plato's *Republic*. You'll sell tens if not hundreds of copies. Or, if your book is about parenting toddlers, and you want to call it *The Catcher in the Rye*, you should also change your name to J. D. Salinger, or Salenger if someone's being a dick about it.

3. **A-Numero Uno Is Money!** The truth is, few people buy books. Even smart people with expendable incomes who "read every day." You think smart people buy things? They're too smart for that! They borrow or steal or go to secret underground smart people meetings where they discuss what will happen to the lower castes. I've been to these meetings. They are a great time. The non-smart caste is too dumb to read much, so don't clutter your front page with whole words or letters. Maybe instead of giving it a verbal title, you should put the Chinese symbol for wealth (subliminal messaging!) or a picture of a naked person on the cover. I'd suggest something from this century, but Rococo nakedness will do.

4. **Stay Positive and Be a Jerk.** No writer ever got a title on a book by just standing around, fingers crossed, praying to the title gods that the publishers like the name the writer gave to his or her terrible, terrible book. You gotta earn their respect. Next time someone offers you "constructive" criticism, tell that person to shut his assface! You're the law in these parts. If someone says the title is not working, punch that person repeatedly. Then ask, "Who else feels like doubting The King?" Positive thinking like that can help you immensely. And now you don't even need a publicist. You

have the most controversial approach to publishing ever. Who in publishing can step to you?

5. **Simple Solutions.** What's the main character's name? Slow down, Dickens! Don't call it that! Instead give people a little puzzle to figure out by calling the book by the main character's hip-hop or porn name (his middle name plus his street name): now your book is called Alexander 32nd Street. Isn't that awesome? It even tells readers where the book takes place. To carry this idea further, type in a random address on Google Maps and go to "street view." What's the name of that deli on the corner? "World Famous Deli"? Is your book about a deli? No? All the more reason to put "deli" in the title, so you invite the deli-loving demographic to enjoy your book.

**SOME GREAT TITLE IDEAS FOR BOOKS
YOU MAY BE WRITING**

Feel free to use any of the following for your book:

Riding in Cars with Goys or *A Room with a Jew*: For Jewish Lit.

The Art of Yielding: What if, instead of baseball, the story was about something less boring? Driver's ed.[7]

Two Hundred Years of Solitude: Remember how everyone loves that book? Well yours will be twice as good with one hundred more years of poignant observations about society!

---

7. I said it again!

As Gay as It Gets: If you write a Jean Genet–like sexfest book or a book about eating more kale.[8]

The Satanic Purses: All the fun of *The Devil Wears Prada* with the added controversy of blasphemously mocking the Qur'an.

The Particular Sadness of Ramen Noodles: A story of your early twenties, way sadder than the *Lemon Cake* book, since not only is your food tasteless and devoid of emotions, but you're eating it alone in a basement apartment at 4 a.m.

Ouch.

A Visit from the Toon Squad: If you write the novelized sequel to the movie *Space Jam*.[9]

---

8. The gayest food.

9. I'd read it!

What Should Be on Your Cover

The art on your cover should be created by someone half your age who works in television and Web design. That's why my cover art was made by a ten-year-old in Indonesia who usually draws logos for Nike. Cover art is updated every two to fifty years, depending on the book.

It's important to understand what makes for a successful cover and what doesn't. To see this in action, here are some examples of better cover designs for well-known books:

A child killing his parents with a knife while they sleep. The blood on the mattress spells "Roald Dahl: *Matilda and Other Novels*."

A picture of nothing because that's exactly what happens in this play: *Waiting for Godot*. Alternate: an audience that has fallen asleep.

A coffin with a body inside and a mirror where the head should be. Yep. You'll be dead soon. Ruminate on that for a day or two: the collected novels of Virginia Woolf.

A Magic Eye that reveals the shape of a man's veiny penis: Anything by Philip Roth.

The ghost of Christmas Future shows a child his depressing future in ad sales after attending Bard College. A pool of the boy's tears form the title: *The Complete Book of Colleges, 2013 Edition*.

Who Should Blurb Your Book

Sometimes people write the words of other people on their books. Normally this would be plagiarism, but if the person wanted to be quoted just to help you sell your book, it's okay. You're going to receive a lot of blurbs, and just in case you were going to get a big head about what famous authors are saying about your book, keep in mind, they didn't read it. If all blurbs were honest, here's what they'd *really* say:

"The sex scenes are reminiscent of old school American fiction—the Puritans, I mean."

"The novel reminds me of *Don Quixote*—in that I felt insane after reading it."

"As soon as I finished I wanted to go back to the beginning to find out why the fuck I read this whole book."

"Sharp, solid, and pointed. The cover of this book is great."

"Right up there with Salman Rushdie and J. D. Salinger (on my alphabetically ordered bookshelf)."

"This book will inspire you to get out of the house and make a difference in the world. That's how boring it is!"

"If you loved *One Hundred Years of Solitude*, you should read it again."

"A real page-turner . . . in that I wanted to finish it quickly so I could read something I like."

"If you read one book this year, then you're like most people I know."

What Should Actually Go Inside Your Book

Now that you've figured out how to hook people into purchasing your book with a title, cover, and blurbs, let's see what you can actually put inside the cover!

First Sentences

First sentences are of the utmost importance. When starting your novel, keep the opening line short and attention-grabbing. The perfect example I have penned is this opening sentence:

"Hey!"

That's terrific! It tells the reader to pay attention and read on because this piece of writing is important. It also sets up the writer and reader's relationship: The reader had better sit down and shut up because the writer is super-aggressive and might have to smack the reader if he or she decides to stop reading.

If this seems too long or confrontational, a better opening sentence would be:

"O"

The loneliness of the hortatory "O" is made even more profound by this sentence's lack of punctuation. It's postmodern writing at its best.

No clear structure, no clear meaning, just a letter. The reader is free to interpret what this sentence is supposed to mean and can spend less time reading and more time thinking about how awesome and simple your book is.

BETTER OPENING LINES

Writers toil endlessly to find the perfect beginning to their stories. Is it provocative enough? Does it reveal anything about the characters? Would it arouse anyone else or should I file it as another "fetish to never reveal publicly"? To help you with your writing process, here are some examples of how opening lines for famous books could have been better:

"Call me Ishmael . . . Actually, just sit there and don't say anything because this is a long-ass story."—Herman Melville, *Moby Dick*

"Mrs. Dalloway said she would buy the flowers herself . . . then she said she might be a lesbian. Then, that she thought suicide was a very brave idea. Boy, when you're inside a person's head, it sure gives away the story pretty quick, doesn't it? I guess that's it, then. Good-bye."—Virginia Woolf, *Mrs. Dalloway*

"I am an invisible man . . . Good thing I found this visible ink with which to write this book—HEY! It's turning invisible! What the devil! Wait—now the ink is reappearing! ACME!!! You've done it again!"—Ralph Ellison, *Invisible Man*

"You're about to stop reading Italo Calvino's new novel."—Italo Calvino, *If on a Winter's Night a Traveler*

"Last night I dreamt I went to Manderley again, only instead of a house it was my eighth-grade gym teacher's head and it swallowed me whole, and inside the house's stomach I met a woman I sort of had a thing for

> back in school, then I woke up thinking my husband was a murderer. But it was just a dream . . . Or was it?"—Daphne du Maurier, *Rebecca*
>
> "In my younger and more vulnerable years my father gave me some advice that I've been turning over in my mind ever since. 'Don't let the door hit ya where the good Lord split ya.' That's sound advice, Dad!"— F. Scott Fitzgerald, *The Great Gatsby*

Writing Prompts

You spend your whole day in front of a computer thinking, *Today's the day this masterpiece comes out,* then you look down, six hours later, and you've written a mess of notes that an insane or high person could write—and did, because you are a little crazy and a little high. If you can't bring yourself to scribble even those crazy notes, here are some prompts to break writer's block:

- Look in the "News of the Weird" section of the newspaper. If it involves dolphins and someone transgendered, you may have a bestseller on your hands.
- Think of a person you really like. Now try to think of one thing that's wrong with him or her. Is it his hair? Her clothing choice? Write until you have made that person despicable in your mind. Make her a neo-Nazi or a cat-murderer. Or pretend the person has killed your only child. Now invite that person over for dinner and write about how that person had no idea you poisoned the food.
- Count the number of people you've slept with in your head. Is that

number high? What is it? Oh, that's not so bad! Write down on a piece of paper who was the best and that person's phone number. Resist the urge to call the person! Now send the number and first name to a good friend with a note that says, "(S)He's yours to take care of now." If you can get little tear specks to hit the paper near the signature, even better. A month later, go on Facebook and look at their vacation photos. Imagine what they're doing together as a couple and how it will eventually be ruined by another person: you. That's what you're going to do! Ruin that relationship, and write the story of how you created then destroyed it!

- Think about a serious drug problem you never had and stories of cops you never fought. Write about them as if you were writing a memoir.

- A picture is worth a thousand words. If you got an advance on a book requiring forty thousand words, all you need to do is find forty pictures and write about them. Or just put them in your book and tell your publisher what they're worth.

- What if Jesus were an alien or a lion? Think about it![10]

- For your second book write a bunch of bad advice to readers and writers in a humor essay. What would that sound like? How would you keep it funny for more than twenty pages?[11]

Now start writing!

---

10. This has never been done before!

11. Please send answers to betterbooktitlebook@gmail.com. Thanks!

How to Write a Bestseller

It's time to cut the shit and get to work on something everyone wants to buy. All you need is a relatable concept or story people would be interested in watching on TV.[12] Ask yourself: What movies or TV shows have really piqued my interest? What horrible event in the newspaper this week would translate well into a movie?

Then, add universally interesting topics: sex, murder, detectives, secret societies conspiring to keep poor people poor and rich people rich.[13]

Write the novel in two weeks. Look up someone who can remodel your kitchen with the money.

How to Adapt a Bestselling
Novel into a Screenplay

Do not read the book! Just ask others who would best play the role, and write for that actor or actress.[14] If you think the movie will do better by sticking to the plot, just reformat a downloadable version of the novel.

---

12. Vampire politics, homicide police investigating a serial killer who is inspired by the Bible, etc.

13. Poor people love plots like this so they can blame secret organizations for their poverty, which is hilariously misguided since the people making them poor are their own congressmen.

14. Bonus points for finding an actor who looks smart enough to discuss in interviews how much he or she loved the book! Richard Gere and Natalie Portman are great at pretending to know how to read.

If the book is written correctly, all you have to do is copy/paste the descriptive scenes and tighten up the dialogue (characters in books mistakenly drone on about one subject for more than ten seconds).

If the book is about unrequited love or a love that never bears fruit, make sure to add a scene where the two lovers get together anyway. People love kissing scenes!

Voice-over should include the opening line of the book so people who tried to read the book think, *This is just like the book!* In fact, just have a famous actor read the entire book and show some related B-roll footage. People will commend you for writing the first movie that sticks to the book completely.

Adapted (and some original) screenplays should only require twenty-four to thirty-six hours to complete. This estimation takes into account food and sleep breaks.

How to Write Award-Winning Literary Fiction

Writing award-winning fiction is just like writing a bestseller, only instead of making the story accessible to millions of people, you purposefully alienate the masses. Then people buy millions of copies and make it a bestseller because of its indie style. Start with a quirky illness or marginalized "other" in society, then add the following universal literary and collegiate interests:

Sex

Murder

Drugs

References to other books about your subject (especially old ones no one likes)

Incessant irony (dramatic or comic)

Meta-stories framing the narrative or a multigenerational story that doesn't focus too much on the main character's grandparents but does spend just enough time that people miss their grandparents and feel some nostalgia for the way people acted eighty years ago.

Futuristic dystopia where the existence of books is threatened[15]

An emotionally unavailable father figure

A fraudulent marriage

If you add these elements and the concept of the book still sounds too interesting to the general population, consider adding more characters or subjects people are squeamish about: gays in the military, transgendered Cub Scout leaders, disfigured war veterans who are also child porn addicts (I'm so torn about liking them!), genocidal dictators, French sexual morality, etc.

Now, instead of spending the necessary two to three weeks writing the book, spend years on the prose[16] so that, line by line, the reader is sucked into a deeper depression with every word. Remember you're

---

15. It's important to make books sound extremely interesting and worthwhile. Remember who you're writing for: not an adoring public, but a bunch of people at the Pulitzer committee whose only job is to read books that deserve prizes for being full of book praise.

16. Fancy word for "words."

writing to destroy not only your own happiness but the happiness of others. You want your book to reflect the yearning and despair of a life ill-lived, which is exactly what you'll know all about if you've spent most of your life reading and writing.

Since misery loves company, you can justify pushing your sad-ass story on other people because often they will find solace in how sad other people feel about reading your book. Two people discussing your book might one day fall in love, then spend the rest of their lives together for no other reason than that your book pulled at their heartstrings years ago. Now they have sad kids who also want to be writers. Look at your progeny of sad people! You are a KING!

Your work is not done. Now you must retire on a farm, where you will never write again. Do not give any interviews until sixty years after your book is published, then tell someone you trust to burn your journals, but wink while saying it so that person knows you actually want your journals to be published so the money can be used to send your kids to college, where they can learn how to trick the system. too. You did it! You're a literary colossus!

Spicing Up Prose: An Author's Guide to Writing a Good Novel

Good authors know that plot is the end-all-be-all of good writing. They also know to keep the movie rights when they finally sell their spy novel. Some people (and by some people, I mean sexually repressed suburbanite married couples) also want to swoon over nice-sounding words, so long as the words are not so esoteric that these people have to look them up in a dictionary. So you must keep your writing simple but pretty. But how can you make the story sound as interesting as the one playing in your brain-movie without using huge words? Easy: Write it better. Here are some simple tips for making your prose better.

Stick to the Story

Many books are deemed classics solely on the merits of their shortness. Do not waste time on character development. Just give the main character a cool name and get on with the constant betrayals and mystery solving.

Tell, Never Show

Sincere readers have grown weary of all this hyped-up realism and use of metaphors and symbols. Make the story short, and don't hold back what any character is thinking, feeling, or the exact way you want the reader to feel about that character. Shorten up the dialogue, and whatever your word count is when you finish your first draft, cut it to a quarter of that number. Now your story should read like this: "My dad was sad. I took him to a football game. He realized that though he was still sad, he had nuanced feelings about sports and being my dad. I love my dad. (This is the part where you feel like my dad resembles your dad and you cry.) Later, he died (cry more, please). Then I was sad." WOW. What an epic! And so easy to read!

Add Some Sex

If you do feel the need to get sidetracked from the plot, there is only one subject worth adding: sex. Even if you're writing about the financial meltdown of the oughts, or forgotten ancient historical figures like Xerxes or Cher, someone in your story (disgusting though it may be) had sex. Discuss how your characters remind you of how certain animals mate. Then describe animals having sex. Clearly this is more exciting than the sexless adventures of Winston Churchill.[17]

When it comes to writing the sex scene itself, start by pretending you've never had sex (for most writers this should not be a challenge), then describe the act as if you were not the same gender as your narrator, add some strange metaphors/sensations that would only make sense if you were in the throes of passion. Finally, include one character who wishes he or she were sleeping with another person at that moment. This will heighten the tension.

Add Ethnic Slurs

Drop four or five of slurs in the first paragraph and people will call you a "brave" writer. Make main characters immigrants without doing any research, or make fun of your great uncle who was Navajo. Try to stay away from the n-word.[18] Make up a few ethnic slurs that characters can call one another, like "twosies" or "slickens." White people will extol your book for sounding "surprisingly authentic."

Add Place

People love hearing about places. Especially places they already know about. The closer to their hometown the better. People love when a writer captures the essence of places they frequent. Usually, you don't

---

17. Imagining him have sex is like picturing the Penguin having sex. I bet he kept his bowler hat on and a lit cigar in his mouth while doing it. Oh, NO! I can't stop thinking about it now! The horror!

18. A word good writers would NEVER use, unlike the small-minded Mark Twain and Harper Lee . . . and William Faulkner, Ernest Hemingway, Agatha Christie, Graham Greene, Rudyard Kipling, Robert Penn Warren, Harriet Beecher Stowe, and many other bad people I don't have room to list here.

have to try very hard to do this. Look up the most common foliage and architecture nearby and mix that into a few paragraphs. (e.g., "The Carpenter's Gothic mansions of upstate New York looked like melting wedding cakes as I approached the ivy-covered college wearing some pants I bought at Walmart in Poughkeepsie where I also saw the following trees: maple, crabapple, larch.") If you're stumped for information, just write about varying weather conditions and repeat the city's name in the sentence. Example: "That wet Seattle rain." If your reader has been to Seattle and it rained there, the reader will recall that the rain was wet and label you a knowledgeable, globe-trotting genius.

Add Current Events

If you can make it seem like your main character is based on a real person, and that real person sues you, you just hit the bestseller list! If you can make up a fake disease that closely resembles a real-life disease affecting people right now, you just hit the bestseller list! If you know of a recently discovered mental disorder that causes strange wordplay, and can merge that character's story with a terrorist attack that just took place, you just hit the bestseller list! By adding real-world buzzwords you can make people feel as though they relate to everything that's happening in your story.

Start with big, sad, nationally recognized tragedies, and people will respond with tender feelings. Then add a few volatile social issues into your scene. Be smart. Be subtle. Allude only when necessary. If your book is about an interracial marriage in New Orleans broken after one of the couple's children perishes in a fire, your scene should look something like this:

> The bed was tattered and shaken as if _Hurricane Katrina_ had been in the room. It was the kind of unkempt room that filled a person with angst. The angst one feels during _an election year_.

"I love you," he said. Where was <u>Obama's hope</u> now? he thought.

She said nothing, and was also African-American (in case I failed to mention that before), so there was some added racial tension to the marriage. She was poor. In spirit and financially. Because of <u>Hurricane Katrina</u> and <u>terrorism</u> and those <u>high gas prices</u> after the <u>Gulf oil spill</u> and the <u>Middle East unrest</u>. She had lost her job as a <u>typing person</u> and now might lose her husband, all because of one fire. The fire that took their son away. She muttered something, then fell silent again.

The room was silent.

The silence felt like <u>9/11</u>.

Optional Step: Make It a Period Piece

You can use the same text as above, but shift the time and place by adding middle school Civil War knowledge. The result reads like an authentic account of life in 1864. The reader will feel as if transported to that tumultuous time:

The bed was tattered and shaken as if <u>Robert E. Lee</u> had just been through the room. It was the kind of unkempt room that filled a person with angst. The angst one feels during <u>an election year</u>.

"I love you," he said. Where were <u>Abraham Lincoln's speaking habits made famous by the Lincoln–Douglas debates</u> now? he thought.

She said nothing, and was also African-American (in case I forgot to mention that earlier). She was poor because she had lost her job as a <u>slave</u>. She was also poor in spirit because the government was run by the <u>Ku Klux Klan</u>. She muttered something about seceding from their union just like the <u>Confederacy</u> had seceded. Then she said <u>"[the n-word]"</u> as a term of endearment for her white husband, which made everyone in the room feel awkward.

The room was silent.

The silence felt like <u>hardtack</u>.

Wow! That was the most authentic period piece written in years!

Optional Step: Humor Book

Ask someone for random nouns and adjectives to finish your hilarious book!

The bed was tattered and shaken as if a <u>fart</u> had been in the room. It was the kind of unkempt room that filled a person with angst. The angst one feels during <u>a fart</u>.

"I love you," he said. Where was <u>Farty McFartpants</u> now? he thought.

She said nothing, and was also African-American (in case I failed to mention that before) so there was some added racial tension to the marriage. She was poor. In spirit and financially. Because of <u>booger-cock pussy-nuggets</u> and those <u>penises</u> after the <u>poop salad</u> and the <u>chunky goat milk</u>. She had lost her job as a <u>poop inspector who inspects people's poop</u> and now might lose her husband all because of one fire. The fire that took their son away. She muttered something, then fell silent again.

The room was silent.

The silence felt like <u>9/11</u>.

Done!

What Should Be Taken Out of Books: Censorship

Before writing your book, you must be wary of using certain words that might offend a fringe group of diligent fun-ruiners who exist in every community. Don't get me wrong, banning all books would be terrific. Then we could finally get back to the only reading-involved activity that brings people together: sexting.[19] These book-haters, however, were put on Earth in order to end the expression of all exciting things.

There is a way around offensive language, and that's to take the dirty thoughts every human has and transform them into a narrative about something totally different and inconsequential. Now kids can read your frighteningly subversive and graphic book. Much like the school systems that devised a way to replace a certain word in Huckleberry Finn with "slave," I will make *Tropic of Cancer* accessible to all ages by ridding it of all the dirty sex talk. The following is an excerpt from the update of Henry Miller's *Tropic of Cancer*[20] in which I have replaced every bad word with the word "potato" or some other food-related item:

> At night when I look at Boris's goatee lying on the pillow I get hysterical.
> O Tania, where now is that warm potato of yours, those fat, heavy peels,
> those soft, bulging potatoes? There is a bone in my potato six inches long.
> I will mash every wrinkle in your potato, Tania, big with seeds from a

---

19. If they could, they'd try to ban sexting, too.

20. Also, I know the Tropic of Cancer is a region of the planet, but some people find the word "cancer" too sad, so I suggest we rename the book *Tropic of Prancer*, then it's playful and has a Christmas theme, so everyone's happy!

*watermelon I just ate. I will send you home to your Sylvester with an
ache in your belly (from eating!) and your potato turned inside out. Your
Sylvester! Yes, he knows how to build a fire, but I know how to bake a
potato. I shoot hot butter onto you, Tania, I make your potatoes incandescent.*

That is much classier.

FAMOUSLY BANNED BOOKS

Ulysses: Banned briefly in the United States for its sexual content. Judge John M. Woolsey overturned the decision, however, after he claimed the book did not give him "even an inkling of a boner."

Animal Farm: Very offensive to pig readers who did not appreciate being portrayed as Russian.

The Da Vinci Code: Banned for being a really poorly written book. Judges around the world heard cases on behalf of the Catholic Church, but no one could finish the book due to "godawful writing no child—NAY! no human—should be subjected to."

Lolita: Banned for its violent ending. Everything else was totally cool with people.

Madame Bovary: Banned for its portrayal of women being free to sleep with whomever they want. This depiction seemed cruel in most countries, since it has never been the case there.

Of Mice and Men: Upsetting to many when one character kills an adorable puppy.

You now have every tool necessary to both read and write a book. Too bad "the book" (as we know it now) is dead. No one will read anything you ever write. I bet most people who bought this book didn't even read up to this paragraph, so if you're reading this right now, who cares? No one else is going to know what you're talking about when you say, "I liked that *How Not to Read* book, but I didn't care for that part at the end where he discounts the entire book and says you shouldn't have read it." The person you're speaking with will stare blankly at you and, realizing he or she is being quizzed in a roundabout way, will say, "Oh, yeah, I didn't like that part either." There you have it. Reading and writing get you nowhere.

You've Done It!

I f you've never finished a book, guess what! You've just about triumphed over this one! Can you believe it? Now all you have to do is wait around to purchase the next *How Not to Read* book. Or, better yet: buy another copy of this book and reread it! What if the next printing has more jokes in it?! Go buy another for a friend! At this rate we will sell nearly three copies! That would be the most a book has ever sold in the history of books. Thank you muchly. Enjoy the rest of your life.

ABILITIES GAINED BY FINISHING THIS BOOK

- Flight
- Stopping time
- Running for public office
- Teaching children the depressing truths you've learned from books
- Never reading again!

How Not to Read: Weaning Yourself Off Reading for Good

Now that you have tried reading, it's time to never read again.

Reading is abysmal. You know this for a fact because you've read most of this book. But how can you leave reading behind when it seems to take up so much of your time now? Every day you want to stop and do something more constructive with your time, but the impulse to pick up a book seems to override your other priorities. I know how it is. You come home from work and you just want to unwind with a refreshing page or two of Weber's *Protestant Ethic and the Spirit of Capitalism*, but all of a sudden you're three hundred pages deep into a Delillo novel, sitting in a park you never remember entering.

You're losing friends. You're losing money. You're putting an enormous burden on your family. It's time to stop doing this to yourself. It's time to change.

Empower Yourself

The first thing to remember is that you're bigger than books. Look at a book on your shelf right now and yell, "I'm bigger than you, BOOK! and I don't need you!!!"

Read Less Every Day

Start small. When you would normally read at work during your lunch hour or read while going for a short drive, stop and consider burning that book in front of other colleagues to show them: "Yes. We can get through this together."

Forget Novels! Stop Reading All Text

No more reading single-word traffic signs like "STOP" or "YIELD." Pick a person whose emails you will no longer read before answering, like emails from your boss or your mother.

Know Your Rights, Fight for Them

If you're in school reading this, there are many ways to inform your teachers that reading is destroying your brain. Show your teacher something from a book you've read that involves racial tension or blunt sexual activity. Now every day is like one big study hall, where the teacher doesn't say anything and allows no reading or questions of any kind.

Help Yourself, Help Others

Now that you've seen the way and the light of a literature-free life, make yourself feel better by freeing others from books. The next time you're in a bookstore, notice that there are security guards and often alarm systems on the front doors. Take a few books off the shelf while no one is looking, go to the cafe area of the store, and throw the books into the trash. Hmm. No one is guarding the trash, huh? Walk out of the store. Return later, repeat.

AGHH! I Finished Reading One Book and Now My Parents Are Forcing Me to Go to College: Surviving the Ultimate Literary World

C alm down! Hey! Calm the fuck down, I said. Listen: You need to think some happy thoughts and remember that this won't last forever. Look at me! It's just a bad trip. You're gonna pull through. Remember: College can be a wonderful place to not read, for a lot of reasons.

If you attend college, you get free food,[1] twelve hours of sleep a day, a constant queue of hot dorm mates who keep saying "I'm just trying to find myself" (i.e., "I'm ready to sleep with a lot of people"), and a chance to redefine yourself as a cool person instead of the guy who threw up at nap time in pre-K. You get to have carefree sex,[2] a chance to meet your potential spouse(s), the chance at a better job just by collecting a piece of paper they hand out at the end, use of a free gym, and you get to visit

---

1. Free, until your first student loan payment.

2. Until your first visit to the free clinic.

with tenured, intelligent, sad, drunk men, who will try to have sex with you regardless of your gender.

Things you'll actually remember from college: You'll have a crazed memory of when John Cage's music and prose poetry[3] made perfect sense to you. You'll also learn a series of small anecdotal pieces of history and literary theory that are tantamount to a party trick: "Homer's *Odyssey* may have roots in Scandinavian mythology" and "Yes, I have heard of Sontag."

Oh, and one more thing. In college, you only stress out about one thing: writing papers. Four years of worrying about organizing your thoughts on a philosopher whose ideas haven't mattered in three hundred years, and that's it! Never again will your life be so free of worry! In the real world, you'll worry about money for the rest of your life, so enjoy this time to worry about utter bullshit.

Daily Needs for Surviving College

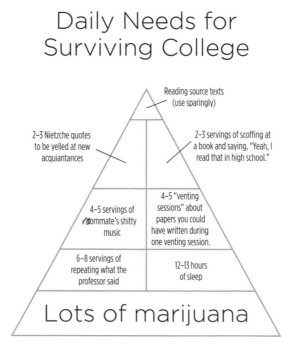

- Reading source texts (use sparingly)
- 2–3 Nietzche quotes to be yelled at new acquiantances
- 2–3 servings of scoffing at a book and saying, "Yeah, I read that in high school."
- 4–5 servings of roommate's shitty music
- 4–5 "venting sessions" about papers you could have written during one venting session.
- 6–8 servings of repeating what the professor said
- 12–13 hours of sleep
- Lots of marijuana

---

3. Like Anime, you'll be obsessed with these subjects for several years, then embarrassed and confused that you told so many people you loved them.

**SOME WORDS AND PHRASES TO REMEMBER
WHILE WRITING COLLEGE ESSAYS**

Teachers love these buzzwords:

Hence . . .

In as much as . . .

The aforementioned argument (it's alliteration and uses up some space that would otherwise be taken up by the rest of the sentence with the aforementioned three words written out)

Not only . . . but also

In conclusion

. . . but rather juxtaposes . . .

I could go on. The point is, college is a big fat cruise that no one has to pay for unless you're a member of the super-rich, in which case, the vacation that is college can last until you're thirty-two.

How to Get on a Professor's Good Side

Academia is a fragile business. Professors know the toil and turmoil that come with writing papers and speaking up in class. Here are some tips for surviving the classroom and using new technologies to your advantage in college:

Learn One Foreign Phrase

Take a foreign phrase from a book and use it every day in class. Better yet, make up a phrase! Instead of *fin de siecle*, say *trompe du leier* and be sure to add a philosopher's take on the book: "Isn't Nietzche's *trompe du leier* very similar to Rousseau's argument here?" The professor will instantly agree. Teachers are always worried that you will find out what frauds they really are. They can't look like they don't know something while taking all of your family's money!

Use Facebook

If your professor is on Facebook, add him or her as a friend immediately. Now post status updates that are hidden from everyone except the professor and say things like "Another four hours of close reading this Roland Barthes book before I start my paper! I <3 school!!" Then, should you ever need more time to write, hire some people through Craigslist and stage a fake funeral and tag yourself in as many photos as possible of you mourning your fake dead uncle. Now email your professor that "something personal came up" over the weekend. He'll immediately check your Facebook profile to see if you're lying. Why was someone taking photos at a funeral? No professor will be bold enough to ask that question.

Ask Questions

This is the easiest way to show you're engaged in the reading. The most simple questions are often the most provocative, such as "What does this word mean that's on every other page?" If you can't think of a question, try a "statement-question" like "I'm just putting this out there, but I found page 63 to be quite interesting." Then turn to page 63 and read the first sentence out loud. The discussion will start moving all because of you!

Never Take Criticism

Remember that no matter what you turn in, your paper is perfect because you wrote it from the heart. The professor's job is to fix typos and underline your most profound thoughts. If a professor gives you a bad grade on a paper, threaten to sue over that professor's prejudice. With any luck, you'll settle out of court and get a passing grade along with a little money to pay back your student loans.

Always Remember You Pay the Bills Around This Place

If there's one place where you should feel entitled, it's college. After all, if there were no students, there would be no school, so show up late to class or not at all, talk during class, and feel free to sleep at your desk whenever you want. What are they gonna do? Give you a detention? There's no such thing as detention in college!

NAVIGATING THE COURSE CATALOG

In case reading the course catalog at school is too daunting, here are some better titles for courses you should take:

"Introduction to Game Theory," or "How to Play Risk and Checkers Better Using Third Grade Math"
Why you should take the class: Fulfills your math credit. If you've seen *A Beautiful Mind*, you've already passed the final exam. Most of the

class explores the theory that chess is a pretty awesome game if you think really hard about it.

Final paper: "Da Mystery of Chessboxin' and Thinking First, Before You Move: Game Theory."[4]

"Freedom of Speech in America," or "There's No Such Thing as Freedom of Speech in America So Let's Discuss It"

Why you should take the class: Though you might think you're expressing your thoughts publicly and people are listening and democracy is prevailing, a guy in a tweed jacket who has never existed in the real world will cite thirty books that tell you you're wrong! Repeat whatever he says in class in your papers: A+.

Final paper: "Whatever You Say Is Right: Why Professors and Other Smart People Are the Only Ones Who Should Have Freedom of Speech."

"Introduction to Insects," or "How Little Can I Do and Still Get My Science Credit Out of the Way While High?"

Why you should take the class: This course is one long episode of *Planet Earth*, only you'll end up retaining strange information about earwig parents who let their offspring eat them for sustenance. Gross! And awesome.

Final paper: "Breeding of *Periplaneta Americana* (Cockroaches) in the Hudson Valley (Specifically, In Our Cafeteria and Dorm Room)."

"History of Cinema," or "Watch Old Foreign Movies and Try Not to Fall Asleep During at Least One of Them"

Why you should take the class: You'll watch thirteen good movies. Worthwhile if you're ever stuck at a party with filmmakers: They'll assume you're cool if you can say anything about Stan Brakhage.[5] Feel

---

4. Most of Game Theory is common sense you could pick up from Wu-Tang lyrics.

5. Remember, you don't have to enjoy the movies in order to hang your great taste over other people's heads.

free to fall asleep during Brakhage's movies and write your final paper on Fellini.

Final paper: "8½ Was Watchable and Therefore the Best."

"Anthropology 101," or "People Are Different but Sometimes Alike; Let's Write Whole Books About This Obvious Bullshit"

Why you should take this class: This class was designed for people who love people watching, then reading about how their people watching differs from other people's people watching. Do not study this subject too long! Years of study will eventually lead you to this conclusion: People are people.

Final paper: "I've Never Been to Africa but There's Some Sexist Stuff Going On There."

"Video Games as Art," or "My Parents Definitely Sent Me to College for This!"

Why you should take this class: Do I even need to explain this one???

Final paper: "Mario Galaxy and Its Roots in Contemporary Children's Movies." That's going to be tough to research!

How to Start Your Own Book Club

Whether they are recently divorced or never married or are secret lesbians, bitter and single women of all types love book clubs. Starting a book club is one of the easiest ways to make friends with the women in your neighborhood. Here are a few tips to make the book club about the community rather than about some book everyone saw advertised on daytime TV:

First: What Do You Want to Get
Out of the Book Club?

Do not start a book club in order to read more! That's not what book clubs are for! A lot of people go into setting up a book club saying, "I'm lonely. I wish these books were real people and that they came with a free bottle of wine." That is a fine reason to start a book club. Perhaps you'd like to get in a verbal argument with a slutty mom down the street but have yet to find the right catalyst for starting the argument. That's a fine reason for a book club, too.

Second: Picking the Right Books

No matter what, everyone will start gossiping eventually. Best to pick a book that leads to the gossip faster. Choose a book with a lot of infidelity or maybe a bitchy character who sounds like someone everyone knows outside the book club. Hopefully that character enters in the first thirty pages.[1] Now start the incessant mean talking!

Third: Have Some Questions to
Ask About Each Book

As mediator, your job is to make sure the conversation never withers. Otherwise, people will awkwardly leave and you'll be left alone in the quiet dark place again where the ravenous mind-mice scuttle through your "blackness feelings" eating up what's left of your sanity. You'll need questions to ask about every book. Here are some titles along with some sample questions I've come up with for you:

---

1. Average completed pages of any book club book.

Virginia Woolf's *Mrs. Dalloway*

1. Is this sham of an existence worth continuing?
2. Seriously, what are we except animals with a significantly larger sense of anxiety about death even while performing menial tasks like buying flowers?
3. Is anyone else having trouble breathing? Not that I can't breathe but that I can't seem to get enough oxygen, you know?!
4. DEAR GOD! Why are we even here?!
5. Throughout the novel, Clarissa seems to like ladies. Have you ever thought about swinging that way? Pssshhh! Me neither!

Charles Dickens's *A Tale of Two Cities*

1. Did anyone get through to the end of the book?
2. Well, can we just talk about the first half then?
3. The first section at least?
4. For fuck's sake, did anyone even read the first sentence?
5. Right. Yeah. Everyone knows that part, Betsy, but what about the rest of the sentence? "It was the best of times, it was the worst of time, it was the age of wisdom . . . and . . . ?" Seriously? All right, who wants cookies?

Nicholas Sparks's *A Walk to Remember*

1. How much weight do you think you could lose if you had cancer?
2. Did cancer help the relationship in this book or burden it?
3. How easy would it be to pretend to have cancer to put that spark back in a relationship?
4. Does anyone know a bribable doctor?
5. I'm serious. I need this. Besides faking a pregnancy or terminal

illness, I don't know how to get a man to stick around for more than six months! Can anyone help me?

Cormac McCarthy's *The Road*

1. What in your life closely resembles the apocalyptic wasteland Cormac McCarthy paints in this novel? The parenting? The houses? What the characters are forced to eat?

2. What else from this desolate world looks exactly like a home all of us saw in real life last Memorial Day? The person who threw a barbecue that was "bring your own beer and food"? Anyone?

3. Who here (Christa, are you listening?), who here has a basement that closely resembles the underground cannibal storage vault the father and boy discover in this novel?

4. Christa, what did you find in the book that stood out to you as "relatable"? Was it the fact that the family sleeps under a tarp? Or that the child gets his nutrition from one can of Coke per year?

5. Christa. We've called Social Services. We're going to use this very book as a description of how you've raised your child. We know this must be difficult for you, but please understand: During the parts of this book where the two main characters travel around with a shopping cart, we thought Cormac McCarthy was actually using your life as a model for his book. You need help. Please stop stealing and hoarding everyone's copy of the book in that Ikea bag.

How a Book Killed My Father

Night. The call came from my mother. Dad was on another trip, a long one.

And this time he wasn't coming back.

I knew the score but I still wanted answers. I felt all knotted up inside, like when the nothingness that was always there suddenly becomes the something you've got to deal with. I knew I had to see him for myself.

My pal Jimmy down at the station gave me a read on the situation. He told me not to sweat it, the same way mom told me never to sweat the small stuff. But hearing that the old man had been murdered wasn't exactly below-the-fold news. Jimmy did me a favor, not telling me the whole story beforehand. That might have ruined it for me. You see, solving a murder is like reading a dictionary. It's full of clear words and definitions, but they don't add up to one single thing. But you can't let that stop you, because there are a bunch of other words you gotta check out just in case they're related, in case they're somehow involved. And you don't stop reading until you hit the Zs and need a nap. But the book keeps getting bigger every day, with more and more words, and if you don't hurry up, some words you thought were pertinent will become archaic and disappear.

When I walked into the old man's study around 3 a.m., it was as quiet as a library. It was a library. But this library had blood on the carpet and one of those chalk bodies the cops are so keen to leave in place of a corpse.

"A paper cut," the morgue doc said. "Biggest damn one I ever saw."

Losing a chick was one thing. Watching someone close the book on you altogether, sure, that hurt. But losing your pops. That's different. That cuts way deeper.

There it was. In all its stale silence: that old leather face staring right at me. I felt like something had just ripped me in two. It was shorter than I remembered.

"Just so we're on the same page, why?" I asked it.

No answer.

"Why?!" I yelled.

It went all quiet on me, like it had lost its words.

I went over and I opened it up. Oh, I opened it up all right. No one was going to take away my flesh and blood without a word or two from me.

I took in the first line, then the next. Then the words just kept coming. I had no idea when it would end. But I had to keep going, never knowing when the next important clue would appear. By morning, I had gotten what I needed from it.

I knew why it had done it, and it was clear this story didn't end at the last page. This story had legs and would soon get away from me if I didn't act fast. Someone had put it up to it. Someone else was the author of this plot. His name was on every page as plain as day.

And I knew what I needed to do.

Day. I was lost in the stacks at Columbia University. I had to do a bit of research on the author that set up my father so nice and neat.

I was alone up there. So I thought. I saw the sway of a skirt disappear behind a shelf. A librarian. Who else would be up here? I walked over. Maybe to talk. Maybe find out what she knew about a certain author. Or maybe just to get another look.

She was in the aisle of old faculty and student papers. The kind that get written just to say you've done it. Writing for the sake of writing. That kind of writing. The writing about books they force you to read in school. Life's kind of like writing those papers on required reading. You have to at least know a bit about the old stuff to skate by in the present. But only knowing a few facts will do the trick just fine.

She was humming something. A show tune. She came up to the fifth shelf, and her legs covered most of the distance. She didn't belong in that gray skirt and brown sweater. She looked like it was her first attempt at trying to belong at this school. Like a Barbie briefly dressed as a college student. I cleared my throat.

"I didn't think anyone else was up here," she said.

"Nor I."

"Can I help you find something?"

"I'm looking for a particular writer. Name of Luke Pierce."

"Oh, I love Luke Pierce! He went to school here, you know! Do you like his work or is this your first encounter with him?"

"We're familiar, but I'm not a fan."

Then she went on and on about why Pierce's books were so excellent. How they fit into the "canon of great mystery writers." The conversation was very one-sided. I occasionally nodded my head like I was listening. Her speech was about as interesting as someone else's diary. She was talking herself into her own web of words. But I kept with her until I could ask:

"What are the best books by Luke Pierce?"

That woman helped me out a good deal with the research. And a few side projects of our own. In the end, I only needed to know a little bit about one book to know what was really going on. It's good she was there to point out which of Luke Pierce's books were the most telling.

Right there in the Columbia Library I read several of Luke Pierce's best books. Some of the texts were frantic. No forethought. Just plot. There was no reason to read a second time. Each sentence told you the author's intention. Here is the first paragraph of Pierce's book *Overdue*:

He never walked during the day. He spent his time in the library wanting to know all he could about books. He spent the days reading and writing, but for every book he finished, a million more were published that same day. It was an endless cycle, and he felt he had not even begun to scratch the surface of everything written before. One great idea finally dawned on him while taking his evening walk: a novel that would take his life to write.

I could read the writing on the wall. It was all spelled out as if I had a confession in my hands. Luke Pierce knew books could kill, and he planted one right for my father the way someone might plant a bomb. If the paper hadn't cut him, the words on the page could have convinced a man to do himself in.

I had him: book, line, and sinker. I felt strange, though. I knew Pierce too well from all that reading. Like he was the hero. As if he were now some dear old friend I'd lost touch with. Shows you how much books can flip you around. Turn you onto the wrong path. Tomorrow I'm meeting with a page at the publishing house. I think I'll write my own story about how easy it is to get information in this day and age.

Just a few weeks later and I had all the information I needed. By then I had given up on reading. It solved nothing. I had lost track of my pal

Jimmy, too. Dive too far in and you leave some things behind on the surface. Them's the breaks. It's best Jimmy wasn't along for the ride. I didn't want to catch any grief for how I decided to end it. It was hot enough out there without some friend giving me the third degree. It was my choice to end it here. And it was my choice how I would end it. Period.

I had Pierce's address. He lived in some small town in Nevada where people were about as sparse as the rain. I drove up to the house in broad daylight. I didn't care if anyone saw what I was about to do. I was justified. I didn't need to cover it. I had this guy's number and his number was up. I turned off the car and slammed the door. Let him know who was here to see him, I thought. I scanned the desert behind the house. I needed to know if he was hiding somewhere in my line of vision. No one. I held my pistol at my leg and walked up to the house.

I opened the screen door and tested the knob. I took the butt of my gun and knocked on the glass. A little harder than the usual knock. I reached through the glass and let myself in.

It smelled musty. Just like the old man's library. I walked through the living room into an office. The only other room was the kitchen, and it looked about as ill-used as the sofas in the living room. The desk had stacks of paper. The bastard's own unfinished pieces. A heavy mass of nothing just waiting to be cut out of whatever book he was working on. A draft came through the window and hit my eyes. I was curious about the writing. I lingered over the desk awhile.

I started reading. Page after page of a style I found painfully derivative. A borrowed bunch of text. Some of the stories I read while standing at that desk were so familiar to me, I felt like my dad was there in the room, reading to me before bed. I finished a fourth, then a fifth story. I looked in the desk to take a breather, and inside were photos that took my breath away. Pictures of me. Of my dad. Pierce had been tracking my dad for years!

I found a letter from the writer's agent offering advice on a new novel. It had the usual encouragements you'd expect: keep at it, you know best, etc. The name the letter was addressed to, though . . . was my father's.

Now I had it. No one was coming back to that house that day. Or ever. Luke Pierce and my dad were one and the same.

What was I going to do? You can't kill a book. People off themselves all the time. Sometimes a book seems like the culprit but it's your own brain filling in the blanks the author left out. Show's you the good a book can do for you. All that time wasted reading. Just to remind you that your thoughts could turn on you at any moment. The answer had been with me the whole time, and now I knew I would never read again. The only books that interested me were by the same man who killed my father: Dad, himself. I had already read enough of those.

Guess I'll go home, and see if there's anything good on TV.

The End.

FURTHER READING

Acknowledgments, or "The Part of the Book That You Probably Don't Care About!"

Neither the blog nor the book would have ever happened without the love, support, and Photoshop training of Anya Garrett. She is a great photographer and multimedia producer. Look her up! (www.anyagar rett.com).

I owe the creation of this book to my agent, who discovered the blog, Courtney Miller-Callihan, and to my editor, Meg Leder, who dealt with many terrible drafts of writing and shaped this into a book.

Thanks also to:

My parents, who still seem to think reading is fun. My brother, Sean, who encouraged me from the start.

The entire Molina family, who seem more excited about this project than anyone.

Adam Newman, who explained to me in under a minute how to make a good Tumblr.

Robert Dean, who helped create my first literary comedy endeavor, *Unquotables*.

Bob Schneider and Peg Haller, Kambri Crews, Emily Gordon, Kent Gowen, Sean Crespo, Carol Hartsell, Rebecca Trent, and Henry Schenker.

Rachel Fershleiser for encouraging me to be part of literary-comedy events (and for supporting all the literary culture the Internet has to offer). Amanda Bullock for helping me put together the first Better Book Club.

The staff at Community Bookstore in Park Slope.

The entire Classics Department at Bard College, especially Ben Stevens.

The New York City comedy scene, which watched me fall flat on my face several times onstage while writing this book (and many times before I had that excuse).

The Blogosphere for being a bastion of creativity, disturbing humor, and (constructive?) criticism. Brainyquote.com for helping complete large sections of this book. Onlineclasses.org for reminding me to put in a glossary of terms section.

The *New York Review of Books*, *Huffington Post Books*, and the *Guardian* for writing plainly about good and bad writing.

Anyone who submitted a title to Betterbooktitles.com! Many people are much smarter and funnier than I. Check them out.

Dan Wilbur is a comedian and bookseller in Brooklyn, New York. His work has been featured on CollegeHumor.com, *Timothy McSweeney's Internet Tendency*, and the Onion News Network. He is the creator of BetterBookTitles.com.